Harry's Last Tax Cut

Also by Jim Weikart

Casualty Loss

Harry's Last Tax Cut

Jim Weikart

Walker and Company
New York

For Lynne

All the characters and events portrayed in this work are fictitious.

First published in the United States of America in 1992
by Walker Publishing Company, Inc.

Published simultaneously in Canada by Thomas Allen & Son
Canada, Limited, Markham, Ontario

Library of Congress Cataloging-in-Publication Data
Weikart, Jim.
Harry's last tax cut / Jim Weikart.
p. cm.
ISBN 0-8027-3212-7
I. Title.
PS3573.E38369H3 1992
813'.54—dc20 91-39724
CIP

Printed in the United States of America
2 4 6 8 10 9 7 5 3 1

▽

1

ENROLLED AGENTS. NOBODY KNOWS who the hell we are. It's just not known like a lawyer or CPA. But, hey, if you want something expert done about your taxes, we're the folks for you.

Carol and I both passed our two-day Enrolled Agent exams at the IRS in the past year. Which gave our partnership some credibility. Harry Sage wanted a piece of it—the credibility, I mean.

I seem to attract more than my share of trouble—tax trouble, that is—and Harry's partnership proposal was trouble from the start. First, he was stupid not to have included Carol. . . .

But maybe that's my fault. I didn't know.

The real trouble started in the wee hours of a Friday morning. My stomach was churning, trying to digest Julia's dinner of *arroz con pollo* and black bean soup, and I had just fallen into a restless sleep when the phone woke me. I flicked on the light, stared at the phone for a couple of extra rings. I don't like phones in the middle of the night. Bad news. It was one-thirty; the last time it rang at this hour my brother was dead.

I picked it up.

"Jay Jasen?"

"Yeah," I said.

"It's Harry."

My stumbling mind tried a mental picture and came up with nothing.

"Harry Sage," he said into my quiet.

"Harry," I said then, seeing him. A big guy with a wide face that smiled blue-eyed, stupidly or sincerely depending on your point of view, blond hair on the long side, and big farmer hands. "Listen, Harry, this isn't a good time for—"

"An emergency has come up, Jay. I have someone here who wants to buy out our partnership. Now. Tonight."

The silence from my end lasted so long Harry must've thought I'd hung up on him. Sure he had sent me a partnership agreement to sign. And sure, he had already signed it himself. But he hadn't had to listen to Carol blasting me—and him—day after day. And I didn't even know enough to tell her what the hell it was about!

"Jay, can you hear me?"

"Yes, and I'm glad you called. I've been trying to reach you for the last few days, Harry. But what I want to tell you right now is that this partnership is off to a bad start. Let's do business from nine to five. I expect your call at nine sharp tomorrow morning. Good-bye, Harry."

And I hung up on him.

But I didn't take the phone off the hook. It started ringing again. I let it go. It rang maybe fifty times before it stopped. Then I reached over to pick it up and put it off the cradle. I wasn't fast enough. Harry was at the other end.

"It's thirty thousand dollars for you," I heard him say.

I sat there on the edge of the bed, hearing that disembodied voice say "thirty thousand" a second time. It was tiny and far away. But clear.

I'd been feeling the squeeze lately, what with the two children inherited from my brother. And thirty thousand bucks wasn't peanuts to me. I gave a deep, deep sigh as I brought the phone to my face.

"Okay, what's up?"

The tidal wave of relief that swept into Harry's voice should have tripped off my alarm system. But he'd caught me tired and poor and I was just listening for the money.

"That's great, Jay. It's best if you come over here. The buyers and I have nearly finished all the paperwork so it's a done deal. Just you is all we need."

"I might have a few questions."

"Whatever, just get over here."

He hung up without saying good-bye and I was left staring at the phone one more time. What had I gotten into?

And it's not that simple as a single parent, getting up in the middle of the night and leaving. You don't leave a seven- and three-year-old even though you know it's ninety-nine percent certain they'll sleep right through the night. As I mounted the stairway to Carol Larsing's duplex apartment, I had real doubts about Harry and his thirty thousand. Was any amount worth another fight with Carol? She was furious about this partnership thing anyway. Would she believe that the thirty-thousand-dollar pot was at the end of this rainbow? Of course there was no question that she was a partner of mine and she would be part of any deal I cut. But what was the deal? How was I going to convince her that we could sell off this partnership deal for thirty grand even though we didn't now what Harry had in mind? I'd have to pretend I believed it myself.

Carol answered after the tenth ring. She took one look at my scowl and beckoned me inside. She has a working fireplace in her living room and it's faced by three large white couches. I stepped past her and had another surprise. A young blond woman was stretched out asleep on the largest couch. She had a sheet wrapped around her but long tanned legs stuck out at one end and a tousled head of hair at the other with an angelic face and the pouting lips of a young Bardot.

"Carol!" I whispered.

She looked around with me and saw that I had taken in the other woman.

"I'll tell you about it in the morning."

That was another surprise because Carol makes a point of not telling me about her personal life although she willingly introduces me to her latest love interest—man or woman.

"What's the deal?" she went on quietly. "It's too late for a social call."

"It's Harry. This partnership we've been trying to reach him about is up for sale."

Carol looked pointedly at her watch. "You've got to be kidding me."

"No," I said, but it was beginning to feel like a big joke. The conversation with Harry seemed hours ago. "Harry woke me from my beauty sleep. He says if I can traipse over to his place now, he's got thirty thousand bucks for my, er, our share of this partnership. I'm broke enough to want to see if it's true."

I paused and although the open-mouthed consternation hadn't quite left her face, I could see a gleam of curiosity in her eye.

"All I'm asking you—for a share in thirty grand—is to come down and watch the kids while I run over to Harry's to collect the money."

She put a finger to her lips and glanced around at the sleeping beauty, then motioned me out the door. I followed her down the stairs.

Without a word of encouragement, but with one sharp look that said I was making a fool of myself, she went on into the office and was wrapped up in a blanket asleep before I'd opened the door to leave.

I grabbed an old leather jacket from my high school days in Ohio and walked the short block along 88th Street to Broadway to hail a cab.

The night air had the feel of the last days of spring rather than the first of summer, quite cool for May. And I had some trouble finding a taxi. I could have walked up to 103rd Street faster.

Harry's office is in a brownstone like mine. Except a stone staircase rises to a second-floor stoop entrance to the rest of the building and to get to Harry's you enter by a gate and go down three steps to an ornamental locked grille beneath the upper staircase.

The grille blocks access to another door that gives entrance to the apartment. I was surprised because both the grille and the door stood open. Light spilled out onto the brown sandstone.

I rang the bell lots of times as though the door weren't standing open. No one answered and I walked in.

"Harry," I shouted, "it's Jay Jasen."

Every light in the place was on. I turned left from the hall into the front office Harry uses for his tax business. Cigarette smoke hung in the air and two ashtrays were loaded.

I shouted again, still getting no response.

Somebody had to be coming back and I sat down at Harry's desk to wait. Just then his telephone rang. Harry's answering machine took it. But I knew it had to be for me. I picked up the receiver, at the same time hitting a button, similar to the one that turns mine off. With his, the recording tape popped up like a piece of toast. I caught it in midair, looked at it, and reflexively shoved it into a jacket pocket as I said hello.

"Jay, thank God," Harry said as soon as he heard my voice. He was sharp and urgent. A silence followed.

"Harry? What's up, Harry? What am I doing here? And why are you wherever you are?"

"There's been some trouble, Jay." He seemed to choke, barely able to get the words out. "Can I ask you to come get me? I need help. It's bad. Real bad."

I'd never heard a man sound so terrible. All my annoyance was instantly gone.

"Where are you? Should I call an ambulance?"

"No, no. No ambulance." I could hear the fear in his voice. "You . . . You come here. Take me to the emergency room. I'm at a pay phone." He choked again on his words. "Riverside and 120th." He started to sob. "I'm hurt bad. Christ, I knew they'd get me. I knew it."

"Harry, I'm on my way. It's going to be okay." I said it as firmly and confidently as I could. I heard his labored breathing ease.

"Are you at my desk?"

"Yes."

"It's in the second left-hand drawer." He stopped and I heard him choking again. Then he went on, his voice getting more and more ragged. "Getting you into it didn't work, Jay. They'll just get you next. Nothing stops. . . . Oh, God, Jay, I—"

The phone clattered. Then it seemed to be banging against something, swinging free. I could hear choking and grunting and sounds of a struggle.

"Harry?" I shouted. I stood up holding the receiver tight to my ear with both hands, my palms sweating and cold. But it became very quiet. Still I listened, hoping, praying, until after New York Telephone asked for one more nickel and the line went dead.

I called the police on 911. A flat neutral woman's voice answered the phone. I was shaking.

"Police operator 275. What's your emergency?"

"A man is being attacked up on Riverside Drive. That's 120th and Riverside. It happened just as I was speaking to him on the phone a minute ago."

"Name?"

"Harry Sage."

"Phone?"

"I don't know," I said.

"You don't know where you're calling from?"

"Oh," I said. I looked down at Harry's dial face and gave her the number.

"Why do you think he was being attacked?"

Come on, I thought, you've got to get to him. "He told me he was hurt. He seemed to be jerked away from the phone and I heard a struggle. He never picked up the phone again."

"Okay. We'll have someone check it out."

It didn't occur to me until after I'd hung up that it was my name she wanted, not Harry's.

He'd said the second left-hand drawer; I looked down at the desk and drawer. A snub-nosed revolver lay in the back with a box of cartridges. I picked it up. It looked clean. Under the gun was a worn black leather-bound address book. I grabbed it too. I stuck the revolver into my right pocket and the black book into the left pocket of my jacket. I left the cartridges behind. On the way out, I pulled the street door closed.

This time I got a cab immediately and the driver was the fastest one in the city. We beat the police to the scene. I spotted Harry lying on a bench in Riverside Park. I asked the cabbie to wait and walked over to him. He was on his side and he had his jacket pulled up over his eyes to keep the streetlights out. I felt a rush of relief followed by anger. The old bastard had pulled one of his tricks again. Perhaps I could get us away safely before the police arrived.

"Come on, Harry, game's over." I shook him by the shoulder none too gently. His body suddenly went off balance and fell towards me. I had to push hard to keep him from rolling right off the bench. And when I did, his head lolled over hanging downwards so I could see the gash severing his windpipe.

The cabbie, watching from his open window, saw me jump back. "What's the matter?" he shouted. "Your buddy dead drunk?"

"Harry's murdered," I tried to say. I couldn't get the volume right.

"Wha'd ya say?" the cabbie shouted.

"Dead. Murdered." This time I said it too loud. The cab driver jerked his head up. "Call a cop, can you?"

He threw the cab in gear and peeled around the near corner leaving me alone with Harry.

I began to shiver and the leather jacket didn't give me any comfort. Harry lay there with his head off the bench and the slit in his windpipe yawning and his eyes wide open. The blood began to run out in a slow trickle where I'd caused the neck wound to reopen and gravity caused it to run toward his head.

I couldn't leave him like that. I cradled the head in my right hand while I rolled the body back so that he was laid out on the bench, eyes staring upwards. My right hand came away wet and I saw it was drenched with the blood. I pulled his jacket up over his face.

Then I stepped back, looking at the body with a second kind of shock. I imagined a knife slipping across my own throat. The idea sent a tingling, icy feeling along my spine and I twisted around. The quiet of being with the body was spooking me.

What had happened to the damn cops? Had they decided it was a crank call?

Covering Harry's eyes let me see the rest of him. His clothes were slashed and bloody, the pockets turned out. Had the killer searched him for money? For something else? The killer must have stabbed him several times. He'd said he was hurt. But he couldn't have spoken with his windpipe severed. The coup de grace was the second round, the one I'd heard. Was it more than one killer? Harry had said "they." Ten minutes earlier I'd been talking to Harry.

"Ten minutes," I said aloud.

Nausea took over. I leaned over one side of the bench and let Julia's chicken, rice, and black bean soup heave out. When I was finished, I knelt, my head between my legs. Then, feeling somewhat better, I retraced Harry's steps to the pay phone on Riverside. A touch-tone phone on a metal pole illuminated by a harsh light. There was a bloody hand print on the inside of the metal weather hood. Harry's? The receiver still dangled at the end of the line. I picked it up carefully, holding it in my clean left hand while trying to dial 911 with a nonbloody finger of the right.

A piercing scream shattered the quiet May night. I turned, dropping the phone, a chill running up from my tailbone to every corner of my brain, expecting to see Harry rising from the dead.

Instead I saw a middle-aged fat woman dressed in a yellow pants suit walking a poodle on a leash.

"Murder," she screamed into her other screams of terror.

She was standing by Harry's body holding up his coat while her dog was sniffing at the pool of blood. Her eyes were fixed on me, and worse, her hand holding the leash was raised and she was pointing straight at me. The poodle began to lick at the blood.

I raised my right hand to calm her and started toward her. The sight of it drenched with Harry's blood threw the poor woman into a new volley of screams.

"Police! Help! Get away! Somebody call the police! Ahhhhhh!"

She stood there frozen. In the distance behind her I saw two men running toward us. And I ran away as fast as I could go.

As I ran across the street toward Broadway, I spotted a police cruiser coming up Claremont with its lights and siren going. At Broadway, I flagged a gypsy cab coming down out of Harlem. I told the cabbie to drop me on West End and 103rd. I kept my bloody hand buried in my jacket pocket and clumsily paid off the cab using my left.

Why hadn't the cops responded to my 911 call? If they had arrived I wouldn't have gotten into this jam. Or would I? But to wait now for the police with that damn woman fingering me invited lots of trouble.

I figured if I went to Harry's I could just wait outside for the cops to show up. Then I could explain the whole thing without that wild woman screaming in my ear.

But a surprise awaited me. The front door to the apartment stood open again. I'd pulled it shut. I gripped Harry's revolver inside my jacket pocket with my bloody hand. Another change: The apartment was dark, the lights out. I had not turned the lights out.

Didn't Harry have a wife? Wasn't there a kid? Would they leave the place open with the lights out?

I stepped inside the door and groped for the switch. I found it and the light flooded the hall and spilled through the doorway into Harry's office. The scene there had changed. Files and tax returns were strewn across the floor. Surprised, I walked in, my bloody hand wrapped around the gun.

Out of the corner of my right eye I saw something moving and ducked. It missed the back of my head but hit hard over the right ear. I fell to the floor and rolled over against the wall. When I looked up, I also came up with Harry's revolver.

A big man, stocky and taller than me with curly black hair and a black mustache, stepped into the light thrown from the hallway. He had a black suit jacket and black turtleneck. He didn't look stupid. In his hand was the remains of the flashlight he had busted up against my skull. Both hands were covered with gray cotton work gloves. He saw the gun pointing at him and his face drained of blood.

"Come on," a woman's voice said. I couldn't see her but her shadow fell into the room as she crossed toward the front door. "Let's get out of here." The scent of a perfume drifted across to me.

Rather than point the revolver, I was so surprised I held it up like a cross to a vampire. He ran. They slammed the door hard on their way out. Then it was quiet.

I pulled myself up against the wall and felt my head. My hand came away with my blood on it. Now I had Harry's blood on my right hand and my own on the left. But I was lucky. If I hadn't ducked I wouldn't have been getting up until morning. Or maybe never.

I looked at the revolver that had saved me with new respect. The chambers were empty. I crawled over to Harry's desk and stood up. The cartridges were still in the drawer. Standing at the desk, I opened the box and took out six. It surprised me how easy it was to load the gun. There was nothing to it. The revolving cylinder flipped out and zip, zip, zip, the bullets went into the chambers. Five of them, not six. That was a surprise too.

I shoved the rest of the box into my pocket and waited at

Harry's desk, clutching the revolver in my lap with both hands. But nobody came back to make trouble. Not even the cops showed up. But waiting like that in the quiet of Harry's apartment with the knowledge of Harry's death on my mind gave me time to think of trouble enough.

First of all, I thought of the big guy and his hands covered with gray cotton work gloves. His fingerprints and, I supposed, his female partner's, could not be found in Harry's apartment. But mine would. In addition, I was the one who had been seen next to Harry's body with Harry's blood all over me just after he'd been murdered. And I had run away.

How could I explain these things? I stopped trying and stood up again, using the edge of my jacket to wipe away at a spot where I'd left some bloody fingerprints. Then I stood there, frozen, thinking myself into a panic.

I could hear the questions an overzealous detective would ask: "Please, Mr. Jasen, tell us again how you found Harry Sage dead in the park? How you ran away? How you came to his apartment without ever calling in the police? How you were attacked by some large man you scared off by waving an empty revolver? While you were searching for what? And what was this partnership that you and Harry Sage maintained? How did it do business? What did it do for business?"

What a fool I'd been! Maybe the whole thing had been to set me up as a fall guy!

Carrying the pistol like a child who has just learned how to carry scissors, I went to the apartment door and slipped on the chain lock. Keys or no keys, they weren't getting back into Harry's apartment without my hearing them. Then I went into his bathroom and washed the blood off both hands, carefully rinsing it down the drain. Next I took the hand towel I used to dry my hands and set about systematically destroying my fingerprints. A rub here and another there. Had I touched the handle of the bottom drawer as well as the second? Hit the hall light switch? Better to be overly careful.

While I worked at removing fingerprint evidence, I looked for something to tell me what Harry's killers had been searching for. The file with our partnership name on it was on the floor mixed in with hundreds of other files. But it was empty and I couldn't tell whether the contents were buried in the mess or gone.

I took a good quick look around the rest of Harry's apartment too. There was no evidence of the wife and kid Harry had talked about in the old days when we'd had a drink after an evening tax seminar. Rather, the bedroom was a bachelor's fantasy. He had a king-size water bed with the same size ceiling mirror over it. A dressing table with a built-in TV, VCR, and CD system lined the facing wall and a ceiling-to-floor mirror another. The dressing tables framed the electronic systems, clearly a man's things, Harry's, on the right. I looked into the drawers. On the left side, there was no evidence of a woman's existence anywhere. No clothes, no shoes, nothing.

In the nightstand I found some smut books and some leather restraining cuffs as well as a roll of leather belts. Under the books was a copy of *Screw* magazine opened to the classified section. An ad for a prostitute was heavily circled in red ink. In it, "Jacqueline" promised that if you came you would come and come again in the plush surroundings she and her sexy young roommates provided. A graphic description followed in the unlikely event you hadn't gotten the message. A picture showed a young nubile body from the waist up, naked, and a delicate face mostly obscured by hair. A seductively open mouth revealed small teeth biting suggestively on the tip of her tongue. I shoved the books and the *Screw* back into the drawer.

The porno books, leather goods, and the underlined *Screw* ad made me feel like a Peeping Tom. I got the creeps. After that I just wanted to get out of there before anyone showed up. I shut off the lights and pulled the apartment door closed behind me. Not that it would do much good, I thought, remembering Harry's stripped pockets. "They" had his keys.

Once outside, I looked both ways to be sure I was alone. I'd been smart enough to take the towel I'd used with me. Now, after I was sure no one followed me around the corner, I dumped it into a trash can and flagged a cab home.

2

ALTHOUGH IT WAS NEARLY three o'clock in the morning, Carol was awake and met me at the door.

"Jay," she asked, "did Harry find you?"

"Yes," I said, but I was shaking my head even as I said it and my body began to shiver as if to project to her that Harry was beyond finding anyone.

"He came here," she added.

I stopped and jerked around to stare at her like a drunken man.

"What?" I nearly shouted and I was moving again, across the hall into the office to my stash of Johnny Walker Red.

"He came here," she said again, following me.

I grabbed the Johnny Walker and set it on my desk. I held up a hand to stop her from saying anything more. She watched me with alarm.

"Jay, are you okay? You don't look so good."

I uncapped the scotch and tipped the bottle up, taking a couple of shots' worth. I shook violently as it went down. Then I sat at my desk, put the bottle to one side, and rubbed my face hard with both hands. I looked up at Carol. She backed away from me and ended up sitting upright on the edge of the brown recliner.

"Harry came here?"

Carol sat back in the recliner then and curled her feet under her. I saw her biting her lip. She nodded.

I stared down at my desk.

"What's wrong, Jay?"

"I think Harry's dead."

"Harry's dead?" She wrinkled her nose at me. She abhors uncertainty. "But you don't know?"

I shouted at her. "Well, he could hardly be dead and come here too!" Then I was shaking my head again. "I saw him on a bench in Riverside Park. His throat was slit wide open."

I stopped and I could see that sinking in. It sank in with me too.

Carol was wide-eyed and she never gets that way. She said nothing. She got up and walked over to peer out onto 88th Street through the slats of the wooden shutters. I think she was trying to convince herself that the world as she knew it was still out there.

"Damn!" she said. She turned around to face me. "He came here right after you left. He seemed surprised when I answered the door. It was as if he expected nobody to be here. He never did introduce himself. He asked if you had left yet and I said you had. Then he said he wanted to pick up the copies of the partnership agreement he'd sent you. I was suspicious and I wouldn't let him in. He looked back over his shoulder, frightened. I said he'd have to get the agreement from you. He said he couldn't wait. That he would come back later."

I squinted at her. "Was it him? Was it Harry Sage? You ever met him?" I tried to visualize poor Harry talking to her with his throat cut. He must have been on his way here as I was going to his place. But why?

Carol rested one elbow in the palm of the other hand and put a finger alongside her cheek, cocking her round face so that her hair made an inquisitive angle to her head. "Blond hair, a big face. Large hands."

"That's Harry." I stood up and took off my leather jacket.

She watched while I emptied the pockets. The revolver, shells, and the black leather-bound book from the second drawer. And even the tape cassette I'd forgotten I'd jammed into a pocket all dumped into a pile on my desk. I slumped down into the chair again waiting for some reaction from Carol. She paced back and forth across the room, stopping at the desk several times to look at the stuff. She had a sweatshirt of mine over the tee shirt she'd worn when she'd come down and it was long and loose enough to play down over her big hips but show off her legs. I wanted to hug her. She selected the black book and began to thumb through the pages.

"All women," she said suddenly.

"Is it?"

"Girlfriends or what?"

I shrugged my shoulders. "Harry told me to look in the second left-hand drawer. But I don't know what he wanted. I found both the black book and the gun."

Carol threw the black book with the other things on the desk. "Whoever they are, I'd say Harry has a woman problem. Why don't you give Bruce Scarf a call and turn all this stuff over to him. He's the homicide detective, not you. All this junk would make him very happy."

I shook my head. "I don't think I can do that."

Carol settled back into the recliner again. "Then tell me what happened, Jay. Tell me all of it." She jabbed a finger at the junk on my desk. "And don't forget to explain where all this stuff fits in."

So I did tell her, trying to remember all of it as best I could. When I got to the part about running away from the screaming lady in Riverside, Carol screwed up her face and stopped me.

"You mean the cops are now looking for you as the murderer?"

"It looks like it."

"And you don't want to clue Bruce Scarf in on this?"

I shook my head. "I feel so dumb. Why didn't I call him

from Harry's? I was so upset I couldn't think. Now I'm too late."

After that she controlled herself until I'd gotten all the way to the end, although she continued to shake her head, flipping her blond shoulder-length hair back and forth. I left out Harry's porno and leather collection. Poor Harry was already low enough in her opinion.

"You might as well type up a confession and run it over to Scarf with all this," she said when I was through.

"I was afraid that was the case. But could you do me a favor and review the same ground for me just so I can see it from someone else's point of view."

"Sure can," Carol said, a mite too willingly to suit my taste. "Jay Jasen is Harry Sage's partner in a secretive business. Harry is killed and Jay is spotted at the scene of the murder. Jay tells the police that he called 911 but just happened to arrive in advance of the cops. But did he call after the murder to cover himself? And why in the world did he say he was Harry Sage? They have tapes of those calls, you know."

"I thought they were asking me for the name of the person being attacked."

"Then you run away from the screamer and *return* to Harry's apartment? Unbelievable. Further, you *tamper* with the evidence by erasing your fingerprints and God knows who else's. Then you return home, having not reported to the police for about an hour since the Riverside Park incident. Now, what if the cops arrive here? They find you with Harry's gun and Harry's answering machine tape. Plus some black book of women's names. You need another person to tell you this looks bad?"

"But I don't have any reason to murder Harry."

"You don't?" Carol went on without mercy. "Why was this partnership of yours with Harry worth thirty thousand dollars? Maybe you'd kill for that. You don't know. It's your share of a drunken agreement, I'll remind you. No reason? Tell me about it!"

I sighed. "Maybe Julia's off the hook. I could ask her to sign up for a twenty-year contract to handle the children while I'm off doing time."

Carol just flipped her blond hair around her neck again and got more serious, which was hardly possible. "Remember, those kids were your brother's, not yours. A family court wouldn't be too sympathetic to having a convicted felon as the parent without a woman in the house. The children could come out worse than you. I don't have to remind you that the final adoption papers have not come through yet. They could be looking at foster homes, orphanages."

Carol had a knack for looking at the grimmest possibilities. Before she threw me into a hopeless depression, I cut her off.

"Just tell me what you think we should do about it tonight?"

Carol said nothing for a moment. "What did Harry say to you again? That part about 'get you next'?"

"He said I was in it now. It wouldn't stop them. They'd 'get me' next."

"Do you think there's anything to it?"

"I don't know. He was very upset. Everything must have been blown out of proportion in his mind. I doubt there's much to worry about on that score. I have nothing such people could use. Nothing at all. Look, they could have taken me out tonight in Harry's apartment if they wanted to get me."

"But," Carol said, holding up a finger high in the air to give it emphasis, "how do they know you have nothing? The man and woman you surprised in Harry's apartment may not have known who you were. Or they might have been different folks. Or you might just have scared them off by waving that revolver." Her finger was now pointing at my desk.

I shrugged. "Maybe."

I put my face in my hands again and rubbed hard. Carol stood up and came over beside me, putting a hand on my shoulder.

"Easy, Jay, I think tonight we can only decide whether or not to call the cops. My vote is no. I think we should wait until tomorrow. If you turn yourself in, they'll just focus on you. I doubt if they can identify you. Certainly nobody's ever going to find that gypsy cab driver. Leave it alone. Sleep on it. Give them a chance to work out other options. See what it looks like in the light of day." She looked down at me and gave me a hug.

She was right, I thought. I was exhausted with shock and emotionally drained. It was better to let it go tonight without some heavy-handed cops pushing me around. They'd probably end up convincing me that I had murdered Harry. In the morning I would remember the facts and Carol and I would make sense of all the chaos.

"That's my vote too," I said.

She gave me a final squeeze and walked away from me toward the door. She was the kind of woman I liked: smart and inquisitive, blue eyes, a round face with a short upper lip, breasts of a Marilyn Monroe, and hips just a bit too large. But her legs could have belonged to a Rockette. When she turned again she saw my eyes on her bare legs. She shook her head in mock sadness.

"Pavlov made a big mistake. He should have used men instead of little dogs."

She didn't speak again until she was out of sight on her way out the door to go upstairs. I thought about the young blond beauty sleeping on her couch up there.

"I'd put on the chain lock if I were you," she called back. "And maybe stack some heavy furniture against the door. Good night, Jay." I heard her locking the dead bolt with her key, leaving me alone.

I trailed after her, closing up with the police lock and the chain lock. Then I pulled the hall table over and propped it against the door knob. After that I went down the hall to the kids' room.

They were sound asleep in their bunk bed, seven-year-old Jennifer up top and three-year-old Dillon below. He was curled into a ball, his gentle child face toward me, dark red hair flopped back on his pillow. I scooped him out. He gave a little stretch and a sigh. He opened his brown eyes sleepily. I sat in the rocking chair and held him, his warm hair against my cheek, and he snuggled back into sleep.

How long I sat there I don't know, but when I discovered my face was wet with tears I carefully laid Dillon into his bed and covered him.

Then I turned the lights on in the front of the house. The TV too. I put Harry's revolver under the spare pillow. Even with all the light and noise and my fears, I was able to get to sleep. But I dreamed of bloody handprints and poor Harry Sage trying to run around and talk to me with his throat cut. I wanted to understand, but the words came out in red bubbles.

▽

3

CAROL'S COMMENT ABOUT A drunken agreement was right on target. The so-called partnership with Harry had started Thursday evening the week before his murder. I had taken the night off from the two kids, from Carol, and to recover from coming off the hundred-hours-a-week tax season.

I had met Frederik Ruscher, also known as Flash, at a place called the Silver Bar Café up north of 110th Street.

Poor Frederik. After the breakup of our country group, he'd left film editing to attempt screenplays. But even with his contacts, he'd only gotten a couple of options. His shoulder-length black hair and beard had shocks of gray and his black eyes under black eyebrows gave off a crazy intensity that made me worry. He had thinned down so that he looked diminished and hungry.

He made part of his living gambling at the Silver Bar Café. They had a bowling machine. A puck is bowled down a short alley hitting some metal levers which determine how many pins flip up. Frederik had become quite good and gambled on his games. His specialty was a variation called Flash, where you timed your puck, hitting the levers with moving lights for the best score. His success led to his nickname.

Flash's success also meant that he didn't have to work while he wrote his screenplays.

And he drank too much.

But I still loved to see him. The conversations always centered around politics, films, novels, and gossip. Frederik did know everybody. And he'd do anything.

Friday night he packed in the bowling so that we could nourish ourselves on Dos Equis, Silver Bar nachos, and vintage conversation.

We'd gotten about two and a half hours into the evening when the vintage conversation deteriorated into a nasty verbal exchange—I don't remember why. I do remember that Frederik aimed his black-eyed, raised-eyebrow stare at me as the best part of his argument. His intensity jumped out and his jaw was stubbornly set.

Then Harry Sage put an arm around my shoulder causing Frederik to break his eyes away from mine to Harry's. With that, he turned away in disgust. "Jay Jasen, Enrolled Agent, I presume," Harry said, still clinging to me. His wide face had a pure blue-eyed smile.

"Hi, Harry," I said. He wasn't somebody I wanted to waste a night off with. I ducked under his arm and closer to the bar with Frederik. Harry came up behind me. I looked around at him. Frederik was studiously looking into his drink.

"Take a look at this," Harry said. He glanced downward and nodded toward his hands, drawing my gaze. And I watched as he fanned a roll of dough that looked to be a thousand bucks in tens and twenties. He thought he was being discreet, but he was drunk and Frederik heard the rustle. He glanced over and saw the money.

"Harry a friend of yours, Jay?" Frederik said.

Harry stepped up to the bar with us, leaning confidentially forward, a sick smile now on his blue-eyed, blond head as if he knew he'd gone too far. He came close to my ear and cupped his mouth away from Frederik.

"It's a new play on the two oldest professions," he said. "I'm making lots of money. Lots of it, Jay. And the women!"

Here he paused to reflect on his good luck. "Lots of women."

Then he stood back a foot but still in my face and looked at me so close he had to shift his eyes to decide which of mine he wanted to look into. He was waiting for me to say something.

"Money and women always sound good to me," I told him. "And to Carol too," I added as straight-faced as I could. "And how about drinks?"

Harry laughed, doing it alone. "Sure, drinks too." He shouted at Jimmy the bartender, then turned to us, uncertain. Frederik helped him out with a cry for whiskey. The signal was out that we were switching drinks.

"Fresh money here," Frederik called down the bar to someone. Out of the corner of my eye, I saw a small-time hood called Chinless George moving toward us.

Harry whispered into my ear again. "I need a partner, Jay. There's a lot more easy money. More women. I need you. It's got to be someone I can trust. And who knows his way around the IRS. It's got to be you, Jay."

"Let's say count me in and we'll talk about it in the morning," I said. And I reached for the whiskey sitting in front of me and clicked the glass to Harry's.

"Fresh money," Frederik said again. He threw his arm over Harry's shoulder. Frederik had his drink in his hand and he touched the glass to each of ours.

"To fresh money," he said, drinking off the shot of whiskey. Then he turned to the bar and shouted, "Jimmy, up again here." He pointed to our three glasses. "And make it four." Chinless moved up alongside.

Harry laughed as if our drunken business deal meant he could relax. We both had tax practices on the Upper West Side. But Harry pushed himself on people. He was socially inept. To me, he was a professional contact—Harry did know his tax code. To him, I was one of his best friends. In the Silver Bar Café that night I went with the flow. This partnership deal would evaporate the next morning with the hangover.

Harry stood close up to the bar and put both his big hands around the fresh whiskey like a hot cup of coffee. His hands reminded me of a midwestern farmer, not a city-slicker tax adviser. And that wide-faced, blue-eyed smile had a boy's innocence about it, but it was on a linebacker's body. Unlike me, or Carol for that matter, he dressed for his financial image, a jacket and shirt from the Madison Room at Barney's and a silk tie with a regimental English pattern. The tie peeked out of the breast pocket. His shirt was open to the third button allowing the light brown hair on his chest to show.

I could see both of us, side by side, in the mirror across the bar. My black mod shirt with almost no collar didn't look professional. But I was taller and not as stocky. And Harry had that look of maleness about him that would sell clothes or beer or cigarettes. He lit up a Marlboro as I watched.

My hair was brown. My eyes brown. Maybe my eyes were a little too close together to look as good as Harry. But he was an ass, not me.

Harry couldn't seem to look across the bar at himself. I watched him find his own eyes there and look away. That meant bad trouble, I thought, but I wanted it to be none of my business.

Frederik placed a hand on Harry's shoulder. "You ever play this game, Harry?" He was pointing to the bowling machine against the wall. Chinless George stood at his elbow.

I'm sure Harry knew both of them and the consequences of playing. Chinless had black slicked-back hair that was too long. And he had a big nose and almost no chin. The big grin on his face nearly obliterated the space between his nose and his neck. He waved to me, ignoring Harry.

"How the fuck ya doing, Jay," he said as a statement. Chinless was always there.

I waved back without responding. Frederik and Harry stood face to face. Chinless came up to me and winked. "Kill two birds with one stone. What a deal. Nuttin' to lose on this one. Do my job and get some bucks from him too."

"Sure, I'll play," Harry said. What could I do but say I was in too? I was the key to the game.

We bowled a couple of warm-up games before Frederik moved us on to flash bowling.

"Hey, whyn't ya tax guys take on Flash and me?" Chinless asked, plastering that grin of his across the bottom of his face again.

"Sure," Harry said, but not me. I looked to Frederik for some help.

He caught my glance and saved me. "We'll play high-low team every game." That meant the high-score player and the low-score player would be teamed together for the next game. And it was the team that won or lost, not me and Harry. I nodded my agreement—and thanks—to Frederik and we played.

The stakes began at a dollar a game. Harry didn't care. When it wasn't his turn to bowl he sat at the bar watching and wearing a big grin as if I'd solved his problems.

Once, while Frederik was shooting, Harry grabbed my arm. "I promise you, Jay. Money and women."

"Couldn't be better," I said as I shook him off. I was concentrating on the bowling machine, trying to keep my score high enough so I wouldn't lose too many dollars. And I'd be damned if I'd spoil my night off by getting into Harry's cockamamy tax scheme—or scam. Because I didn't give a damn.

Chinless had the biggest laughs and the smoothest scores. He acted as if this was the best game he'd ever had going. But since I'd heard his gambling war stories, I knew it wasn't true, even discounting half his other tales as lies.

Later—very late—after the hour hand passed 1:00 A.M., I decided to quit. I'd won ten dollars and everybody else was a loser, so it was pretty even. I stood back at the bar having one for the road Frederik insisted on buying and watched the other three play. Chinless quickly switched it over to "middle man out." Frederik or Chinless would win and the other would be second and out and Harry would have to pay off. Except I knew Harry would be allowed to win sometimes. Now that I was gone, Harry became fair game.

I wandered out onto Broadway and across the street to an all-night coffee shop to start the sobering-up process. It was a slow place and I wasn't functioning well, so I was there longer than I meant to be. When I came out intending to walk the twenty-some blocks to 88th Street, I saw the three of them standing in front of the Silver Bar Café. Harry was hailing a cab. Lacking any judgment, I shouted at them to wait. But I was across the street and they were drunker than I was. They piled into the cab and it pulled away from the curb, racing off downtown, the cabbie and my buddies oblivious to my shouts to stop.

I walked—if it could be called walking—all the way home and fell into bed to sleep it off.

▽

4

SURE, I HAD A Saturday-morning hangover. Good God, after all that beer and whiskey. But it didn't stop me from getting up to handle my parental responsibilities. Jennifer had a West Side Little League game at one o'clock. She and Dillon were bouncing on my bed between eight and nine. They dragged the poor cats in and out. The television is in my bedroom so they had the cartoons on too. I drifted in and out of a fuzzy-headed sleep. At ten after nine I gave up on it and dragged myself out of bed. I'd taught Jennifer to twist the coffee machine dial to the On position if she got up before me, and times like this I could give her an extra hug. The hot coffee was waiting and I poured myself a good cupful.

Jennifer plays first base for the Zebras, a peewee Little League team sponsored, of course, by Jasen & Larsing Tax Associates. The kids were always excited on days Jennifer had a game, but this Saturday things didn't work out. By noon a light rain was falling and the phone message came around: The game was rained out. Personally, it was such a light rain I would have played anyway. But some Little League mothers, always protective.

Anyway, the rain didn't stop me from finding a rental car and taking the kids to Peconic Bay. After the children's parents died and the summerhouse in Massachusetts fell apart, I found this good deal on a place. It's isolated and on the water. And I figured I owed Jennifer and Dillon the country freedom they had gotten used to.

By the next Tuesday morning both the hangover and Harry's proposal were an indistinct memory.

That Tuesday was normal until the mail arrived. It was a good day for Carol and me to get work done since the rain came down in torrents outside our windows. A dining-living room combination, just off the entrance hall of the brownstone, had been turned into our office. Tall floor-to-ceiling windows looked out on the street and on a garden in back. Equally tall French doors with frosted windows separated the two spaces. They could be closed for privacy or left open to work together. On Tuesday morning the doors were open. The doors into the hallway which also serves as the client waiting room were almost always closed. We don't let the children's cats, Snow Ball and Tiger, into the office. Too many clients are allergic to cats.

Carol and I didn't have any appointments, but we were climbing out from under the many extensions we had filed which were due on August 15th. August seemed a long way off for both our clients and us. The good side of May and June is that we recover from the tax season.

Carol was working on a robbery casualty loss evaluation for the Jacobsons. She was checking to come up with the greatest possible fair market values of the stolen goods. The IRS always audits big robbery losses and tries to knock them down. Carol wanted to start at the highest point so the client would end up with an adequate value for the theft after the knockdown.

I was puzzling out the amount of depreciation a writer named Brender had taken for his home office during the years before he sold his brownstone. About midmorning Jennifer opened the door and asked if she could come in. Julia had taken Dillon out to the park and Jennifer was bored.

"Sure," we both said in unison. We needed the break and

Jennifer came in carrying a book she wanted read to her. She was home from school with a head cold she got from playing in the rain at the Peconic Bay house. Her brown curly hair was held back with two of the rainbow-sprinkle barrettes she loved, but the cold had knocked the twinkle out of her blue eyes. Wearing flannel pajamas with little teddy bears all over, she hopped up into my lap. I started to read the adventures of a girl carried away by a talking kite.

That was the scene on a rainy Tuesday in May when Carol pushed aside her theft loss evaluation and fished the mailbox key out of her desk. She was gone long enough that I had gotten halfway through Jennifer's book.

When she came back she was waving a legal-size document. "What's this?"

I looked up at her. "One, it's a test of my eyesight for fine print being waved at twenty feet, in which case I fail. Or, two, I don't know."

She wrinkled her nose at me and, coupled with the way she swung her blond page boy around her shoulders, I knew she was upset.

"Then I'll tell you what it is," she said angrily. "It's a partnership agreement. A guy named Harry Sage says you're going into business with him. Since I thought I was your partner, I'm a little upset."

Carol sat emphatically in her desk chair and swiveled to face me. She pushed the chair so that it rolled back from the desk and it appeared she was going to go on through the windows into the garden. She wore Levis, and her Reeboks walking shoes gave her more grip on the floor when she pushed off than she had expected for her little demonstration. But she didn't flinch, keeping her blue eyes right on mine.

I threw up my hands, dropping Jennifer's book.

"Hold on, Carol, I can explain. I saw him on Friday night. He had this fantasy that he and I would be partners. I only played along because I didn't want to put up with him. Talk's cheap. Sometimes it's easier to say yes than no. You are my partner and I'm not making deals behind your back."

She kept nodding her head in an "okay, but I don't believe it" way.

"Look I just never mentioned the deal to you because I had forgotten the conversation had taken place."

She waved the partnership form again. "Harry Sage didn't forget." She pointed towards the bottom of the form. "He's hot to trot. He's not only signed it, but his signature is notarized. Now he wants you to do the same and return a copy. He doesn't even ask if you approve. It's a given. Then he'll file it with New York City."

Jennifer was wearing her rabbit slippers and now she began to kick lightly at my desk with a swinging foot. As I sat and thought, I smoothed back her hair but she didn't stop.

"That's enough," I told Jennifer.

"What was it that actually happened?" Carol asked, but I recognized it as a demand. I racked my brain trying to lift the fog that had settled over the conversation with the drinks and bar bowling machine on Friday night.

"He gave me no details, Carol. Just some mishmash about wanting me in as a partner. He claimed he had something new going where we'd make a lot of money. That's all I remember."

Which wasn't quite true. He'd said something about lots of women. But I didn't think it would be constructive to tell Carol about the women part.

"I told him it sounded good to me, that's all."

Carol shook her head sadly. "It's dangerous to let you out alone on a Friday night, Jay. You and I have spent several years building up a nice client list of writers, editors, artists, and filmmakers. But any given evening you may jeopardize it all with a drunken agreement."

Now I frowned at her. "A drunken nod is not a contract."

"A *man's* word is no longer binding," she muttered under her breath.

"Come on, Carol," I shouted at her, now glaring myself.

"Read, Dad, read," Jennifer was saying. She had gotten off my lap to pick up the book. Now she was holding it in front of me as she tried to climb back onto my lap. She smiled easily, her blue eyes recovering the twinkle I hadn't seen yet this morning. But I ignored her.

"You're just not being fair. The way to solve this is to find out what Harry Sage is offering now that he and I are both sober. We can tell him that the agreement has to include you." Then I thought about the women part. "That is, if we wish to have anything more to do with Harry Sage and his offer."

"That's exactly what we'll have to do," Carol said rolling her chair back to her desk so she could bend over the agreement. "There's nothing here to describe the business Harry's offering you. Just a fifty-percent interest in return for your goodwill and equal time." Then she added, "Nothing but this covering letter."

She walked across through the French doors and handed me the letter. I nearly fell off my chair. The letterhead said Jasen & Sage, Tax Investigations. It had his address but two phone numbers. One was ours.

"Let's get hold of the son of a bitch," I said, "the faster the better."

Carol paused, acting uncertain, but I knew she was pressing home her point. "Should I call? I'm not even mentioned in this deal."

I stood up and Jennifer looked up at us. I took the book from her and handed it to Carol "Here. Read Jennifer's book to her and I'll make the call. That is, if you'll trust me to." Jennifer's winning smile had now given way to a questioning frown as she looked from one to the other of us. Carol winked at her.

"Okay, I'll call Harry Sage," she said. "If only to get him over here to read your book to you, Jennifer. After all, it's expected of all the partners."

"Carol!"

Not even looking back at me, she picked up her phone and dialed. Meanwhile I told Jennifer to watch daytime television—an unheard-of concession—until Julia and Dillon came home. But she was learning fast. She also negotiated Heavenly Hash ice cream for dessert plus a promise to finish the book at bedtime.

As Jennifer ran out to head for the TV, Carol was listening on the line. "It's an answering machine. The voice is a woman's, but it sounds as if she's agreed to let him call her *girl*."

From her tone, I knew Carol didn't like Harry's attitude toward women. And I was going to take more of a beating.

"This is Jay Jasen's business partner, Carol Larsing. We need more details on this partnership offer you've sent us. Give us a call. Make that ASAP, okay?"

She gave me a severe look. "Harry will have to make life-threatening changes before he could be a business partner of mine."

I agreed with Carol. I pushed the Jasen & Sage, Tax Investigations partnership papers to one side and began to shuffle into the tax work on my desk.

Carol, surprisingly, went back to work too. "What do you think we can get away with for the value of a two-year-old mink coat taken in the robbery? She bought it originally for five and a half thousand."

"I don't do minks," I said without even looking up. I found the Brender return again with its brownstone sale problem and began working.

That night Jennifer got her Heavenly Hash and her full complement of daytime and nighttime reading and went to sleep pretty happy for a kid with a head cold. And Dillon, no slouch, cashed in for a free ride on her deal.

Two days had gone by with no word from Harry. Then he'd called me at one-thirty in the morning. And ended up dead, before I knew who the buyer was. Or, for that matter, what the so-called partnership did for a business.

▽

5

As I SAID, I got to sleep after Harry's murder with the lights on and the TV blaring and the gun under the pillow. If you can call watching nightmares sleep. I rolled and tossed until dawn broke outside my window. Given primeval reassurance by the light of day, I turned off the lights and TV, and fell into a deep, dreamless sleep.

I overslept. I awoke with two children and two cats bouncing on my bed. My hand closed around Harry's revolver under the pillow before I caught myself.

"Wake-up time, Jay Jay," Dillon said. Poor little guy, at three years he already had to wear glasses and he had them on. "It's wake-up time. Ten o'clock."

Snow Ball purred into my right ear. I groaned and lay back down into the pillows. Ten o'clock was the only time Dillon knew, so I wasn't alarmed. I cautiously felt the lump on my head where I'd gotten conked with the flashlight.

"Come on, Jay," Jennifer said. "I'm late for school and we had to move all the stuff to let Carol and her friend in."

The news that Carol had arrived made me sit up and try to shake the cobwebs out of my brain. It had to be late. Yeah, nearly nine o'clock. Jennifer would be late for school. But Julia could take her.

Julia stepped through the front door as I came out of the bedroom. She only weighs about ninety pounds, but then so does a wildcat. From Latin America, she has black shoulder-length hair, black eyes, and black-rimmed glasses, and she doesn't reach the five-foot mark.

I pulled up short. She looked me up and down, me in pajamas, bloodshot eyes, and disheveled hair. Then she gave me a look of moral disgust.

"Jennifer is late for school again, yes?"

I stood my ground, hopefully sounding authoritative and confident. "We've had a real emergency here, Julia. Up all hours. Could you get the children something to eat and then take Jennifer over to school?"

She threw up her hands.

Passing her, I tripped on a corner of the foyer rug. It made me look as if I lurched past Julia, confirming her worst suspicions. I walked the length of the hall with her eyes boring into my back. I caught a glance of Carol and her Bardot-look-alike friend as I passed the kitchen door.

Getting myself cleaned up and composed took some time. Julia and the children had taken over the kitchen and Carol had moved with her coffee and toast into the front office. I ended up in the office too, to avoid Julia, arriving with coffee and a plate of buttered and jellied toast. And I had Harry's gun, carrying it at the small of my back under my shirt.

"This is my sister's kid, Charlene," Carol said. Charlene looked right at me. She had tan eyes that went with her tan face and blond hair. I swallowed hard.

"Hi, Charlene." Her lips pouted at me as she said hello. I sat at my desk, the gun hard against my back.

"You must be from Minnesota," I went on stupidly.

"Yeah," she said. "I'm doing some job hunting. Aunt Carol's doing me a favor and letting me stay here."

She finished her coffee and bounced up on her long Rockette legs—the legs must run in the family—and moved to the door.

"Nice meeting you, Jay," she said. "I gotta get going to

meet a friend down in midtown. I'll catch ya later."

I waved as she went out. Then I turned to Carol and put the gun on my desk. I saw she had several newspapers discarded on the floor by her desk.

"Harry made the local radio news," Carol said. "WINS and CBS and Imus in the Morning."

"Yeah?"

"But only the murder. Nothing new for us. And the *Times*, *News*, and *Newsday* have nothing on it this morning."

I pointed to Harry's stuff on my desk. The black book was missing. I looked over at Carol and saw that she had it open in front of her.

"What's happening?" I nodded toward it.

She reached out and snapped it closed and threw it across the room. I caught it and put it on top of the revolver and the answering-machine tape.

"I started fifteen minutes ago and dialed ten numbers. Six no-answers, three busy signals, and one angry, irrational man who never heard of Bobbi and told me never to call there again."

"Hmm," I said through a mouthful of toast. I sipped at the coffee.

I absently picked up Harry's book. Yes, all women's names, every one. And first names only. He had started with Ada, Adele, Adrianna, Ann, another Ann and then Anne, Bella, Bobbi, Bunny. . . . Every page the same thing, first names. I counted and got to a hundred names at a third of the way through. And not one man. I put the book down.

"Busy boy," I said. Carol made a noise in her throat that I wouldn't have wanted to hear if I were Harry.

Then she became very businesslike. "Okay, Jay, let's go over what we have. Start with why you have those things of Harry's on your desk."

I looked over Harry's stuff and my memory seemed to be as clear as a bell. "Harry called when I was at his desk." I pointed to the cassette. "That popped up when I attempted to shut off the answering machine. It was accidental. Later, when he was talking to me, Harry asked, 'Jay, are you at my desk?'

" 'Yes,' I told him.

" 'The second drawer,' he said. At that point Harry's troubles began. When I looked in the drawer, I found the revolver and the address book. I took both and went to find Harry."

Carol wrinkled up her nose in disgust. "I think he wanted the gun. Typical male attitude."

That made me mad. "Hardly typical, Carol. He was murdered a few moments later."

She nodded, stood up and walked over to my desk, picking up the black book to flip through the pages.

"Wow, it's a lot of names. Even for a severe case of satyriasis."

"Satyriasis?"

Carol looked disgusted again. "If I said male nymphomania you'd know exactly what I was talking about, wouldn't you, Jay?"

I threw up my hands. "I know what satyriasis is. But I just think you're jumping from conclusion to conclusion without any real facts. What's eating you, anyway?"

Her lips made a thin smile then and she looked down at me. "I'm sorry, Jay. Between Charlene showing up, Harry's deal . . . I'll stop jumping to conclusions."

"Well, you may be right. Harry had a weakness for women. Any time I met him for a drink, if anybody in a skirt made eye contact, he'd be gone. From what I saw in his apartment, his wife is gone too."

"Maybe she wised up," Carol said. "But if he was such a philanderer, maybe he just kept adding women he met to this list." She flipped through the pages one more time. "Yes, these entries are all in different pens and pencils. And some are crossed off." She looked back to me. "I know you said you were drunk when Harry cut this deal. But can you remember anything to give us a handle?"

I had to think about it. "Damn, no. He really said nothing. I wish I had asked him."

Carol walked over to the brown recliner and sat down,

never taking her eyes off me. "Tell me as much as you do remember."

"He said he was rich and flashed a big roll of cash." I hesitated and Carol could sense that I was thinking of equivocating. She raised a hand and waved me toward her.

"Come on, Jay, everything!" she said sternly. "This isn't gossip we're talking about."

"Well, he, ah, he said that I should see some of the women he was getting into."

Carol shook her head in disgust.

"Yes," I went on, the memory coming back. "He made a bizarre statement which I've just thought of. He said, 'It's a play on two of the oldest professions.' And he had to have me as a partner because he could trust me."

"He's never seen you out drinking for a night off," Carol muttered.

I ignored her.

"Did he say, 'two of the oldest' or 'on the two oldest'?"

"I can't remember. I think 'on the two oldest.' "

"Well," she gestured toward the black book again, "women and the oldest profession is obvious."

I nodded. "It would appear so. But he did say the play was on two professions."

Carol held her chin in her right hand. "Did anyone else hear the discussion or did he talk about it with your buddies?"

"Not that I know of. Frederik was there and a gambler called Chinless George. Chinless must have had to talk to him about something because Frederik and I stayed away from him."

Then I stopped because I remembered something else. "Later, very late, I left alone and went across the street for some food. I took my time—"

"—because you were too drunk not to—"

"—and when I came out, I saw them flagging a cab, the three of them. They all must have been really loaded. Maybe Harry did give something away to them. He was loose enough by then."

"Maybe they were just going home."

I shook my head. "No, Frederik lives on the corner. In fact, let's give him a call right now."

I picked up the phone and dialed Frederik's number. The line was busy. Carol had picked up on her extension.

"It doesn't mean he's on the phone," I said. I looked at my watch. It was ten minutes to ten. "He just leaves it off the hook when he's been up all night bowling for dollars."

Carol came over and took Harry's cassette tape. She snapped it into our answering machine and pressed the rewind button. In a few seconds it stopped and she pushed the play button.

"Elementary," I said, watching her in amazement.

The first three callers hung up. Then came a guy checking out meeting Harry for an IRS audit date. It was for today so Harry wouldn't be showing up. Finally, there was a message from a woman with a deep throaty voice, saying she was Donny and to please call her. She left no number. She and the audit guy were the only two messages.

I flipped through the book and found a listing for a Doni, one *n* and no *y*. Nothing made her name stand out. I picked up my phone and dialed her. I let it ring ten times before I hung up. Carol had her extension to her ear and hung up with me.

"I thought we'd get more out of that tape," she said.

I opened the bottom drawer to my desk and dug into the chocolate chips I keep there. Carol went to her desktop humidor and took out a Havana cigar. A friend in Switzerland sends them to her. She says a good cigar helps clear the mind. That may be, but it does nothing for the air in the office. Still, after a bad night's sleep we hadn't yet gotten off square one and she was welcome to all the help she could get.

But I quickly tire of cigar smoke, even though I close my door and she has a fan that vents it out the back. I wandered down to the children's room. What I needed was a little walk and talk with Dillon. He was playing with an armless doll which had belonged to Jennifer, riding it on a plastic horse. Snow Ball sat a few feet away watching.

"Hi, Dillon," I said, sitting cross-legged on the floor beside him. Talking to Dillon clears my head. He always has a fresh perspective. A walk in the snow on Riverside the day after my brother died had started our talks.

He smiled, brown eyes behind diminutive glasses.

"Hi, Dad," he said, getting to his feet. He varied between calling me Dad or Jay Jay. This time he picked a good time to come out with Dad. I needed it.

"What are you playing?"

"Horsy. You want to play too?"

"Sure."

Dillon passed me the second-best horse and I picked out my own doll rider. Then we went galloping across the red carpet of the children's room.

I find the truncated and mutilated bodies of their doll world humorously ironic. When I play with the kids, I stumble through a land of missing arms and injured eyes, finding a litter of doll bodies hidden under pillows and in mattress crevices. Jennifer laughs aloud and Dillon doesn't understand that my play differs from his.

But this time, I picked my doll rider for physical completeness and it rode safely behind Dillon's lead.

'You feel like going for a walk?" I asked Dillon after a few minutes. He jumped to his feet and went running for the door. I had to hurry to catch up. He carried his horse, and so I brought mine as well.

Outside it had turned into a perfect day. The sun had warmed everything and a clear blue sky formed a stunning backdrop. Dillon and I raced each other across 88th Street to the Sailors' Monument in Riverside Park. We took our time then, walking down into the park to the community flower garden and then on to the playground. We left our dolls and horses in sight by the sandbox and headed to the swings. I was swinging Dillon when I got down to business.

"We have a big problem."

"Carol again?" he said without even looking back at me.

I admit I was very surprised. Maybe Dillon was getting too old to talk to seriously anymore. He was beginning to understand what I was really talking about. Carol had been the current subject of my little talks with him.

"No, not Carol. Fooled you this time." I gave him a pat on the head as the swing came back.

"Push harder, Dad," was his response and I gave a shove that brought a squeal of delight.

I liked being a father to the two kids. How much I enjoyed it was a surprise to me. And they gave back as much as I put into it and more. Coming home to their attention buoyed me up more than anything I could remember.

"Tell me what I'm going to do about this mess."

"Mess?" Dillon looked over his shoulder with a worried expression as he swung away and came back again. He thought he had made a mess.

"Not you," I said, laughing at him and getting a smile as a reward. "It's me. I'm a silent partner in a deal with a guy named Harry. That's what I thought, but now he's the silent one."

I brought the swing to a stop and Dillon jumped down and went running to the sandbox, his red hair flopping in the air behind him.

"It's Harry's fault," I shouted, running to catch up with him. "I'm no more than an innocent bystander. Harry's the one who has something to hide. But he's gone and made me look like I have everything to hide. And I've made myself into the fall guy."

Dillon turned back to me looking concerned. "You fall, Jay?"

I stared at him. "Maybe, little guy. Maybe Carol too, I don't know."

Dillon picked up his horse and doll and started trotting them around the sandbox.

"I just never thought of myself as good at murder and intrigue. I get this trembling of the nerves I can't stop." I held out my hand and it had its own tremor. I didn't have to exaggerate. "I'd rather just be keeping score. But right now I'm a player and it's bad guys, one; good guys, zero."

"You want supper for your horsy?" Dillon said. He was presenting a handful of sand to his horse and he turned to offer some to mine. A tiny kid like Dillon wearing glasses makes him especially cute—and vulnerable.

I laughed and trotted my own horse a little closer, but I also glanced at my watch and saw that lunchtime had arrived.

We walked back slowly, holding hands. Dillon chatted about this horsy and the horsies to come. I said nothing more. But these therapy sessions were always useful to me.

Julia was waiting for us at home. She beamed with approval as she always does when I relate to Dillon *man to man*. Little does she know that I am the principal beneficiary. She took him in tow and I headed back to the office. Snow Ball tried to follow me, but I shoved her back gently with a toe until I got the office door closed.

▽

6

CAROL HAD GONE. I opened all the windows and turned her fan back on to dump the lingering cigar odor.

Yes, maybe I would fall. And the best I could do was to sit tight and wait.

I settled back into my swivel chair and pulled out the Brender tax file to do something useful. The dumb guy had sold his brownstone in the same year he'd earned an extra one hundred thousand dollars from a screenplay. Why couldn't he have sold it in the prior year when he'd had a loss? He probably wasn't even going to get a replacement residence, so that all the work I'd done figuring out his office-in-home capital gain would come to nothing anyway. Well, it was now down to putting the figures together and letting the poor fellow know the extent of the disaster. And then moving on to the other tax work stacking up on my desk.

I was just transferring Brender's numbers from Schedule D and Form 4797 to page one of his 1040, only fifteen minutes from completing the whole return, when Carol came waltzing back into the office. She was distracted and didn't see Tiger sneak in behind her. I forgot Tiger myself when she plopped down a copy of the *Post* over Brender's return. She had it open to a page-four headline:

TAX MAN MURDERED

A vicious mugger attacked tax accountant Harry Sage, stabbing him repeatedly until dead and robbing him. The murder occurred on Riverside Drive near Grant's Tomb. Police were looking for a young white or Hispanic male wearing a black leather jacket. A woman surprised the assailant and he fled toward Broadway.

There was no reference to the ransacking of Harry's apartment. Had the police kept that quiet? Or didn't they know yet? Harry wasn't pretty enough to rate a picture.

I raised my eyes from the article to Carol.

She swung her head back and forth as she spoke. "Well, so she got the brown leather jacket as black and thirty-six-year-old you as young. It's surprising she got the male part right."

"Thirty-six is young."

She ignored me. "I think you ought to call Bruce Scarf. The *Post* report means you have a public source about the murder. Just don't tell him anything more than you've read in the papers."

Poor Bruce. He was supposed to be a good friend. But here I was calling him in his professional capacity—a homicide detective in an East Side precinct of the NYPD. And Carol, as always, was right. I could get him to nose around with his West Side friends in homicide.

Bruce is very big and very black. In size, he looks much like the boxer George Foreman. And Bruce, once a boxer, had won a few fights in Golden Gloves competition himself. I met him during the sixth game of the 1986 World Series. He and I were both losing a lot more than our shirts going into the tenth inning until Bill Buckner blew Boston's win over the Mets by letting the ball roll between his legs. We were at the West End Café—the old West

End—and bought the bar a lot of drinks after the win.

Bruce was in and took my call.

"Hey, what's happening, my man?" he said in a voice that matched his size. "How's my main woman?"

I glanced up at Carol, who was still hovering over me.

"We're doing all right," I told him glibly. "How about yourself?"

"Could be better, could be better. Little emotional problem I'm working on at the moment. I think she's going to be okay, though. You know what I mean?"

Bruce was always getting himself into emotional jams. He made his own trouble, always falling in with a woman who was hooked up with somebody else.

"Good luck, Bruce," was all I could say. Then I went on. "Listen, I've got a problem—rather, Carol and I have a problem. We thought you might be able to help us out."

Bruce chuckled. "Help Carol? You think I'm crazy, man?"

I took that as his normal joking around and couldn't tell him it wasn't funny. I stumbled onward. "There was this guy named Harry Sage—"

"Yeah. He's one of ours now. Accountant. Right. Murdered last night over on your side of town. Dude a friend of yours?"

"No, no, no, not my friend. He had offered me a business deal. A partnership. Kind of pushing himself onto me. I just wanted to know what's happened. Have you guys put the cuffs on somebody, or what? You know what I mean. Whatever you're entitled to tell me."

"Sure, babe, it's a West Side case but I'll check it out. Get back to you later. Take care, Jay."

"Take care." Funny how the old sign-off sounded as if he knew more than he was telling me.

"He's going to check it out," I told Carol who had restrained herself and not listened in. She nodded and then went out to the bank.

I picked up Harry's book and dialed Doni's number again. On the third ring a woman picked it up.

"Doni?" I asked. Tiger had curled up under my desk lamp.

"No, Doni isn't here anymore, dear." Her voice had a hard, brittle edge to it. "Somebody else do?"

"Do you have a number for her?"

"No." She was firm.

"I'm a friend of Harry Sage. Doni was too. Harry was murdered last night."

There was quiet at the other end of the line.

"I'm going to give you my name and number. Please find Doni and ask her to give me a call, okay?"

"Harry's dead," she said as if to herself. "I'll try," she said to me.

After that conversation I moved the *Post* off the Brender return and actually spent a half hour finishing up his taxes—at least it was all done but the photocopying and collating when the phone rang. And I left Tiger sleeping on the desk.

"Jay Jasen?"

I recognized the throaty voice even though I'd only heard it once on Harry's tape.

"This is Harry's friend, Doni. I have a message you've been trying to reach me."

"Did you hear about Harry?"

"Your message said he's dead." Her voice had become soft, almost reverent. "But I just spoke to him yesterday."

"Maybe you didn't see the papers today. He didn't just die. Someone murdered him."

"Murdered him!" There was a catch in her voice now. "Why would anyone murder Harry?"

"I can't figure it out. I was hoping you might know."

"But what happened, what happened to Harry?" She sounded like she was fighting for control.

"It's ugly." I waited.

"Yes," she said, but it sounded small and fearful.

"Someone stabbed him to death. They slit his throat."

"Oh," she said, making a noise like a stomach punch blowing the air from her lungs.

"You were close to Harry?"

Her crying was like a sighing in the wind and then she hung up on me. I stared at the receiver and then hung up.

I found I was shaking and I sat there unable to grasp anything that was happening. This was far beyond my control. The doorbell began ringing. I thought that somehow Doni had arrived to get at me. I ran to the hallway door and looked out through the foyer windows into the vestibule. I could see Bruce Scarf standing there, waiting. And Carol was just coming up behind him.

"Shit," I said aloud. My heart skipped a beat. Make that five beats. A homicide detective can have that effect if you're wanted for murder.

I raced back into the office and scooped up Harry's revolver and cartridge box and deposited them into a drawer, nearly slamming it on my fingers.

"Look," Carol said, as they came in. "I found Brucie on our doorstep."

Bruce had on a white silk shirt with the cuffs rolled back and a black tie loosely knotted, allowing an open collar. His trousers were black too, and neatly pressed, and he wore a Western belt buckle honoring Black cowboys in Nevada. I knew Bruce had his piece in a small black holster strapped to the ankle of his black leather cowboy boots. He wore darkly tinted glasses so, as he said, "I can look real mean, like an urban trooper." A gold pendant around his neck behind the tie said Maria.

"Hey, my man," he said as I stood up. Even as he grabbed my hand and gave it the double shake he always used, I moved away from the evidence still on my desk—a black book and a cassette tape. He grinned, showing very white teeth like a Cheshire cat.

He looked back over his shoulder at Carol. "I see you still associating with *that* woman."

"I still here, big boy," Carol said.

Bruce laughed deeply. "Well, woman, it sound like you been taking some lessons on how to talk right. Maybe I get you to come around to my point of view."

Bruce saw Tiger sleeping on the desk and stepped over, putting out his big hand to pick up the cat.

"Watch—" I began.

"Don't—" Carol piped up. But we were too late. Bruce jerked his hand back as Tiger let out a hiss and slapped at him with her claws. She missed him, but came away with a little piece of his white silk shirt. I think Bruce would rather lose a piece of skin.

"Man, that's a killer cat you got there."

Carol was smiling. "Only takes to the family. That's why we don't let her in here."

I carried Tiger to the door and set her out in the hallway.

Examining his sleeve, Bruce sat down on the edge of the brown recliner. Then he looked from me to Carol.

"Well, what the fuck, you got some beer? Or a man gotta bring his own anymore?"

"No, no, don't move yourself, Brucie, I wouldn't want a *man* to do anything he didn't have to," Carol said. She left us.

"The real stuff," Bruce shouted after her. He laughed and shook his head. "That woman's really something, ain't she, Jay."

"And Harry Sage," I said nervously, "what's that look like?"

"Ah! Well, that one looks pretty tight."

Carol came back carrying a Beck's for Bruce and Amstel Lights for us. I sat at my desk and she took the couch.

"Pretty tight?" I echoed, surprised. Had the cops got this thing tied up already while I was worrying my guts out? "You've made an arrest?"

Carol looked as surprised as I was.

Bruce examined his bottle and drained half of it. The gold Rolex on his left wrist caught some light as he raised the beer. "No, no. We got a witness but no suspect in custody. It's a matter of time, though. It's gotta be a mugging attempt gone bad. A bad reaction when he didn't cooperate. The witness says it was a young white male wearing a black leather jacket. The lab report confirmed he's Hispanic. We're tracking him down through the usual channels. We'll pick him up soon. You can bet on it."

"Hispanic?" I said.

Bruce looked from me to Carol as if wondering what our problem was.

"Yeah. Seems the perp tossed his cookies at the scene. No stomach for his own violence. The lab analyzed it as rice, chicken, and black bean soup. You tell me, don't you gotta be Puerto Rican to eat that shit?"

"Or Cuban," I said.

"What?"

"Jay said 'Cuban,' " Carol said, almost shouting.

Bruce laughed hard again in his deep bass voice. He stopped and polished off his bottle. He held it out toward Carol to replace. "I know why Carol wants us to pick up a Cuban."

"Oh, shit," I said.

"Why's that, big fella," Carol said.

"She think there ain't no Cubans in this country but those fascists run away from Fidel. She want us to pick up a fascist."

Scarf always overdid his accent to bait Carol. He laughed hard again. She hadn't taken the empty bottle. "You want me to correct your point of view beginning with the English?"

"That woman's crazy, Jay. One minute she's trying to learn the jive; next she's way out of line."

Bruce got to his feet. "I know where the fridge is. Don't bother." He disappeared out the door. Carol and I looked at one another, neither one of us saying a word until he returned.

I got the conversation back on track. "Anything else about the Sage deal?"

Bruce sat down on the recliner again, this time letting it fold out under him so that he was comfortable. He examined the new bottle and drained a third of it. Then he looked at us.

"Oh, sure. Here's a good one for you. Nothing to do with the case, really. A funny story. Sage's pinky on his right hand was amputated—sliced off. It must have happened when he held the hand up to protect himself. But nobody found the finger. Officers at the scene found a fat lady in hysterics. Her dog was lapping at the guy's blood. Get this. They figure the dog ate the damn finger!" Bruce made a face that must have gone with Carol's and mine. "Good story, huh?"

"I'm glad you told it," I said, "but I think it might make me sick." Bruce thought I was kidding. "Anything else about Sage himself?"

"Let's see. I did take a couple of real notes." Bruce reached behind to a hip pocket and pulled out a small notebook. He flipped it open and looked into it. "Here we are. His wife's name is Judy Sage. They'd separated. The secretary in his office is Fran Pappas. But that's stuff you got already, right?"

"Yeah." I mentally noted the names as he said them.

He put the notebook away. "That's all I got for you. Sorry it's nothing you don't know."

Did he have more he wasn't telling me?

"Thanks. I owe you a drink. If I pick up this guy's business I'll owe you two drinks."

Bruce got to his feet. He peered into the bottle and drained it, setting the empty on my desk. "I gotta get going. I was at the Two-oh so I thought I'd see you." He walked over to the door. I got up and followed him. He turned to face me as I opened the street door and looked me up and down, shaking his head. "You just can't get enough trouble, can you, Jay? Take care, my man. And take care of my main woman there too, you hear!" He shouted the last line and was gone before Carol had a chance to respond.

I closed the door after him and went to my desk, scribbling down the names of Judy Sage and Fran Pappas before I forgot.

"Wish he hadn't told me that stupid finger story."

"Just like Scarf," Carol said. "And, by the way, you didn't tell me you barfed."

I looked up. She was sitting on the edge of her desk looking at me.

I just shrugged.

"Well, thanks to Julia's cooking, Bruce and his buddies are way off your trail. But if they ever get to you, you're a dead duck. The black bean soup would nail you.

"But maybe Julia would be willing to perjure herself about what she cooked. But if she's caught too, who would take care of the children with both of you in the slammer?

"Of course," she went on, "if they're out looking for this fictional Hispanic character you've created, they're not looking for the real killer either. We're on our own."

Carol had been flipping through the Manhattan phone directory while she talked. She pointed into it.

"I don't find a Judy Sage, but here's a number for a Fran Pappas up on 123rd Street."

She read it off and I dialed. As it started ringing, Carol picked up on the extension. After ringing twice, we got an answer.

"Hello?"

It was a flat, nasal female voice.

"Fran Pappas?" I said.

"Yes?"

"Fran, this is Jay Jasen. You worked for Harry Sage, right?"

"Oh? Oh! Yes. Poor Mr. Sage."

Carol, listening on her extension, put her hand over the mouthpiece.

"That's the voice on Harry's answering tape."

"Listen, Fran," I went on, "Harry was setting up a partnership with me. Did you know about that?"

"With you?" she said slowly. "Yes, I remember something about that. Mr. Sage sent you some papers last week. Right?"

"That's right. Look, I want to get hold of Harry's wife. Do you know where she is?"

"Oh? She's crazy."

"Crazy?"

"She lives with those Moon people up on 107th."

"Moon people? You mean Reverend Sun Myung Moon's people?"

"Yeah, that's it. Hey, do you think she killed Mr. Sage?"

My heart skipped with a little flutter. I remembered the woman's voice in Harry's apartment. "Why would she do a thing like that?"

"Why? Well, you know the divorce hadn't gone through yet. They were fighting over custody. Mr. Sage wanted to get the kid back. Hey, she would have done anything to keep the kid."

"Harry's kid?"

"Oh? Yeah! Little Harry junior. He's a real cute kid. Just finishing second grade."

"Just one more question please, Fran?"

"One more? I guess it's okay."

"Did you see the police today? Did you go to the office?"

"Yeah, Mr. Jasen. I was in the office until I found out about Harry, er, Mr. Sage being murdered and all. Then I came home. I couldn't stand it—being there in his office with him dead. He was so *nice*, Mr. Jasen."

"And the police?"

"Oh? That's how I found out. They came to the office this morning. I told them Mrs. Sage might have done it—murdered him. Do you think it was all right to tell them I thought she did it?"

"You have to help them," I said trying to sound neutral. "What else did you tell them?"

"What else? What else could I say? I didn't know anyone besides Judy who'd want to kill Mr. Sage. Judy Sage is a terrible person. And crazy. He told me all about it."

"And the police? Did they, ah, take a look around the office?"

"Sure, they looked in the files and everything. Harry, I mean Mr. Sage, must have left in a terrible temper last night. I bet *she* called and got him to meet her and riled him up with some junk about the kid. He'd left a mess behind you wouldn't have believed. Files thrown all over the floor!"

I found myself nodding my head but I couldn't tell her I'd seen it for myself.

"Sometimes he did that," she went on.

"What did the police say about the files?" I asked her.

"Oh? The files? Well, I'll tell you, Mr. Jasen, I'd just gotten it all cleaned up when the officers arrived and told me about the murder."

Carol was rubbing her free hand across her eyes. I hoped Fran didn't think too much about the long silence at our end.

"Hello? Mr. Jasen? You still there?"

"Yes. It's okay. Tell me, Fran, could you help us out again? I mean now. I mean, work for me? For Harry and me? Continue to go into his office until everything's straightened out? I'll pay you."

"Oh? I don't know, Mr. Jasen. I feel so strange there, what with Harry dead and everything. Oh, it's so terrible." She started to bawl.

"Hey, take it easy," I said. "I'm sure Harry would want his son to have the best deal. How about for him?"

She stopped bawling as fast as she started. "Okay, Mr. Jasen, I'll do it. I got nothing else to do now, anyway."

"That's the spirit. Take off until Monday. Then go in like normal. I'll call you there." I thanked her again and said good-bye.

Carol shook her head slowly. "Poor woman."

"Which way do you mean that?"

"Every question was a surprise to her. Harry had her wrapped around his little finger."

"What can I tell you? Her cleaning job saved my tail."

"And that's probably all we can expect from Fran, to save your tail. She doesn't have the consciousness to save her own."

"I've learned never to underestimate a woman," I said but I was sorry I'd said it as soon as it was out of my mouth.

Carol growled but said nothing. I'd pay later. I kept my mouth shut until she spoke.

"Well, it leaves us with Frederik and Judy Sage as the only known leads we have yet to talk to."

I didn't tell her about Doni's call because I was reaching for the phone. Frederik's number rang this time. But nobody was answering. As for the Moonies, neither Carol nor I nor New York Telephone could find a listing for their house on 107th.

Carol got to her feet and came to stand by my desk. I have to admit she looked as though she didn't know what to do next. She thought for a moment, running her tongue along her upper lip. "Tell you what. I think I'll just walk up to 107th and see if I can find Judy Sage. I've seen the Moonie house there."

I was nodding as she suggested it.

"Yeah, I'll go up there and talk to Judy Sage. Better me, since she doesn't sound like she's going to be real hot on men after Harry. And if I appear at their door, I'll surprise the Moonies and get them to produce her."

"That'd be great."

When Carol said walk, she wasn't just referring to getting some exercise. She has a phobia about riding in a car, subway, or even a bus, although she has been known to take a car ride in an emergency and does take a bus more frequently than she used to.

She ruffled through the papers on my desk until she came to the two copies of the partnership agreement. She pushed one toward me and handed me a pen.

"It would be hard to argue we have a partnership agreement without proof," she said. "I want a signed copy to take with me."

Reluctantly I signed under Harry's signature and, at Carol's insistence, dated my signature the same day as Harry's. As a notary, Carol witnessed it as that date also. My mother used to call the process putting fat on the fire. Then Carol made some photocopies of the signed agreement. She kept one and handed me the rest to file. I shoved them under the Brender tax return on my desk.

Carol gave me an encouraging smile and I saw her to the door. She walked briskly toward West End Avenue and disappeared around the corner.

7

I WALKED SLOWLY BACK into the office and got Harry's gun and cartridges out. I sat at my desk, staring at Harry's junk. The phone rang and I picked it up. "Why would they murder Harry?" she asked without even saying hello, a throaty, soft voice.

She caught me, I have to admit. I found myself considering her question, trying to find an answer. I ended up just echoing her question.

"Why would they murder Harry, Doni?"

"There's no reason. It's gratuitous violence. New York City."

I paused again. "What if I told you it wasn't a random act? That Harry was murdered for a reason?"

"A reason for murder? What is it?"

"He was very upset yesterday. But I don't know why. If you were close to Harry, you know things that could put this together."

She started to cry. After Fran Pappas's heavy-metal bawling, her crying sounded like a Brahms symphony.

"I'm sorry," I said. "I wish I could tell you that it's going to be okay. But I'd be lying. But I'm truly sorry."

She was quiet, collecting herself. "I want to talk about Harry. Can we meet?"

I'm lucky to have a strong heart. "Sure, anytime. Even right now if you like."

"Yeah, now's good. If you could make it right away. Can you come to Johnny's Place. It's on East 60th between Lexington and Park. One o'clock too soon?"

"I'll be there."

"Just ask the bartender for Doni."

"And I'll be a clean-shaven, brown-haired guy with a long-sleeve pink shirt."

"And you can look for bracelets."

I was elated. At last I would talk to someone who knew Harry. I went to the kitchen and poured myself a glass of cold milk. Dillon was still there eating his favorite, a blueberry yogurt. Since Dillon gets exuberant with his food, I tried to be affectionate without getting too close. But he got one twenty-five-cent-size blue daub on my pink shirt cuff. I cleaned it off the best I could, laughing. Julia clicked her tongue at Dillon's sloppiness but had a smile on her lips. I rolled my cuffs back.

I went out and grabbed a cab on Broadway and made it to Johnny's Place at two minutes past one.

"Doni?" I asked the bartender.

He waved his hand toward a table out in their sidewalk café.

I went outside and there was Doni. She had frizzy brown hair—the kind she couldn't do anything with but she made it look like that's what she wanted. She wore round wire-frame glasses. Her skin was naturally dark or maybe she had an early tan. She had on a light green silk jacket and a white silk dress underneath with a scoop neck, an abundant woman but without fat. Someone who fights herself to the point of doing six miles a day of walking or running to keep everything under control. It was all well under control. The jacket had shoulder pads—but she didn't need puffing up. She stood as I approached, giving me full view of an extremely attractive woman of five-eight or five-nine.

She had said to look for bracelets. And on her left arm she had gold bangles—one, I guessed, for roughly every year of her life, thirty or thirty-five of them. She had dangling gold filigree earrings and silver rings on several fingers. A necklace of small jade masks mounted in silver was set off by the light green of her jacket. Her eyes were golden brown behind the wire rims, now red from crying.

Her face had an open erotic promise to it, full-lipped, with a slight puffiness under the eyes. Harry had told me he would get lots of women. I wondered why he wanted lots if he had one like this. And why did Doni, sexy and graced with the ease of a gazelle, fall for Harry?

"Hello, I'm Jay Jasen."

Although she had stood, she did not extend her hand, rather she nodded as if to say, "Of course you are," and gestured silently to the chair across from her. We sat.

She had a Bloody Mary that she hadn't yet touched and I ordered the same.

"Tell me everything," she said. "I want to know what happened to Harry."

Her voice was richer and even more attractive in life than on the phone, a deep, throaty voice I'd only heard in the professional singers who were my clients. Doni's was very sad.

I shrugged. I wasn't about to tell her everything. "Did you see the *Post?*"

She nodded.

I opened my hands to show that I knew nothing more.

"How well did you know him?" she asked.

"I have a tax business like Harry's. We met in a corporate tax course at NYU about six years ago. It was at night and we'd go for a drink afterwards. We got together off and on since our offices were on the Upper West Side. And you?"

She paused and I had to wonder what she was thinking. "Harry and I had a date about two years ago. Last year he helped me work out a big tax problem. We spent a lot of time together and got to know each other well—" She stopped suddenly.

"You loved Harry?"

Her eyes filled with tears. "We didn't start that way. His marriage was breaking up and he needed somebody just to be with. I did too. It went from there."

"He never said anything that might indicate someone was angry enough to want to kill him?"

She shook her head.

"I don't think I know anything to tell you. It's astonishing, but you see, I barely knew him—I mean his real life outside his time with me. I knew he was getting divorced. I knew his business was taxes. We had some lovely times.

"Whether they catch the guy or not," she went on, "won't bring Harry back. Why would I know about some killer described in the *Post*? Sounds like a ghetto kid out for a quick buck and, knowing Harry, he wouldn't give it to him."

I could have told her it wasn't some ghetto kid but that was the one thing I wasn't telling anyone but Carol. But if I couldn't get Doni around the prima facie evidence, how could I drag out the truth? I didn't know the questions. Was she also dancing around me?

"Listen," I said, "Harry sought me out last Friday night. He offered me a business deal and I foolishly accepted."

I stopped. I was backing myself into a corner. Harry thought the partnership was his trump card. I shouldn't squander it. Especially since I didn't know how to play it.

"Ah . . . someone gave Harry an offer of sixty thousand bucks for our partnership just before he died and I don't know who might . . ."

My voice died in my throat as Doni's head snapped back as if I'd slapped her and she sucked air in through her teeth. She jerked to her feet and I gasped. She was slimmer than I had thought, big but no fat at all. The brown frizzy hair would look great splayed across a pillow, the glasses off.

"So that's it," she said, her voice having that deep throb even in anger. "You're really here to track down the mystery buyer so you don't miss out on making money off Harry. That's disposing of Harry as fast as you can. Don't give me this friendship shit. You didn't give a goddamn about Harry."

"Wait—"

She cut me off with a wave of the hand. "This was a mistake. I can't help you close your deal. You see I have to go through a painful emotional process. And now I understand I must do it alone. Lovers and dogs have one thing in common. We're never mentioned as survivors."

I stood up in a panic. "I'm sorry," I said awkwardly. "But you've got it all wrong. I'm frantic, but not for cash. It's because the guy who offered Harry the sixty thousand may have murdered Harry in lieu of purchase. I'm looking for the buyer because if he finds me first he may extract the same purchase price from me. He may kill me."

I extended a hand but she pulled back instinctively. "Please," I said.

She seemed to relax then, as if I'd solved a problem for her. As if I weren't a dangerous man anymore. It struck me that she had thought I killed Harry and now she decided for sure that I hadn't. She sat down again and so did I. She took a sip from the Bloody Mary and looked around. I did too. The other diners had returned to their food.

"I'm sorry too," she said in a low, breaking voice. "I'm very upset. I can't think about Harry. Give me a little time and space. Maybe I'll think of something. But I can't believe someone would do that to Harry. Not for a stupid business deal."

She stood up again and I bounced up with her.

"Give me a day. I'll call you then, even if it's to tell you I have no second thoughts, okay?"

I nodded to her. There was no other way I could play it.

She pointed to my sleeve. "You should have told me about that." I looked and saw that the cuff had fallen out and Dillon's blueberry yogurt stain was visible. "It's a perfect identifying mark. No one else has one."

I smiled. "My kid did that to me after you and I talked on the phone."

"Kids? You're married?"

"No, no. Not married. Just two kids."

"That's good," was all she said and she smiled for the first time, showing bright white teeth. And if she'd had any doubt left, the thought of the children dispelled it.

Women feel that way about me. They see me as more secure—and less threatening—because I have kids.

We said nothing more as I walked her to the sidewalk. I flagged a cab for her to cover my awkward feeling.

"I'm sorry about Harry," I said as the cab pulled up.

Doni put a hand on my arm, catching the bare skin just below the sleeve and leaned toward me. She was close, and the scent she wore came to me.

"In a way I'm glad, you know," she said. "I had to get Harry out of my life. He was from the past and no good for me. Now it's been done for me. I'm thinking of the possibilities."

But her eyes filled up with tears as she let go of my arm and got into the cab. As I watched her go, I thought of the possibilities. But just then I identified the scent. It was from Harry's office, worn by the woman with the guy who had smashed me over the head.

"It's nothing to do with this damn book!" Carol threw the black book at me in disgust as I came in. I caught it in midair and laid it on my desk.

"Well, that's something. How'd you find that out?"

She looked sheepish. "I reached seven women. None of them ever heard of Harry Sage."

"Mmm," I said. I knew I had to let her finish raving before I could drop Doni on her.

"A couple even laughed in my face and hung up."

"Carol, your feelings are hurt!"

She blushed.

"Yes," I continued, "let's say these women are professionals. They probably think you're the wife or girlfriend checking out names and numbers in the old man's diary. If they're good, they don't talk about their clients, just like we don't talk about ours. They're not going to give you a thing."

I could see Carol didn't like the idea of not being trusted by other women.

"You were probably right about the gun," I said to make her feel better. "Harry wanted the revolver when he sent me to the second drawer, not the book. Phone numbers couldn't stop the people murdering him, no matter what attractions he may have had for these women."

She kind of grunted.

"And," I said, dramatically raising a finger, "I've just come from meeting with the only number we did reach. With Doni."

"She's probably the exception that proves the rule," Carol muttered. But then she realized what I'd said and looked over at me.

"Okay," she said, "and I'm back from the Moonies. Maybe we both have stories to tell. But I want to know if we did get something out of this book, so you go first. What did she tell you?"

"She was his lover."

Carol wrinkled her nose at me in surprise. "His lover? Then she knows everything."

I shook my head at her. "Harry doesn't seem to give out facts to anybody."

"And?"

"She was very upset. She couldn't see how she could help. But she's going to think it over and give us a call. That's all there is."

"And was she a prostitute? A streetwalker? Was she a high-class call girl?"

I shook my head again. "Not for my money." I remembered Doni's brown frizzy hair and all her bracelets. "No. She was his lover."

"Damn book," Carol said again under her breath. She hadn't gotten over the refusal of the women to talk to her. "It's just women he got it off with one way or another. Or prospects." She got up and paced around the room once as I watched her, her blond hair swinging around her shoulders.

"Okay, okay," I said, "let's get off the book. I've given you what Doni said. Now what about Judy Sage and the Moonies?"

A smile passed over Carol's lips and she went to her desk, picked up something, and dropped it on my desk. A set of keys.

"What's this?"

"She gave me the keys to Harry's. It means she'll deal."

"Well, that's great news. Tell me what happened. In fact, let's get down to basics. She kill him?"

"She didn't volunteer and I wasn't asking. Cooperation was what I was after and cooperation was what I got."

"Just like that?"

"I went right up to the door and rang the bell. One of Moon's Korean front people answered the door and showed me into a little reception room. She left me for five minutes to stare at Moon's smiling face covering the walls. Then Judy came in closely tagged by two Moonies. The American one was her legal adviser. The Korean one smiled like Moon himself, but never said a word. But I got a feeling he was making all the decisions at some subverbal level and, also, was there in case I got violent.

"Judy was all smiles, not the grieving widow. I couldn't decide if the smiles came from a deep religious belief that Harry was in good hands or simple relief that she was rid of him for good. She had those dark circles under her eyes the Moon followers get when they are pushed with that keep-them-awake technique."

"Hey, maybe the smiles just meant she was happy she'd gotten away with murder when she saw the *Post* story identifying a killer."

Carol shrugged that one off. "There was nothing I could give them except the business angle. I showed them the partnership agreement signed by Harry and you. They took the copy. Then I told them we were interested in the tax business. Judy could have cared less. But the American adviser liked the idea of us offering to buy Harry's practice."

"Buy out his whole practice? We never discussed buying out the practice."

She screwed up her eyes at me and shook her head once in despair. "I had to use a little creativity to get them to deal, Jay. Come on. He was itching to get hold of Judy's assets for the Big Guy. He kept trying to put words in her mouth. Finally he just said, 'Give them the keys.' The big Korean smiled and nodded as if he didn't understand a word of English. But I didn't buy that."

Dillon pushed open the office door and came running in to jump up on my lap. Jennifer, just home from school and thus the excuse for this interruption, followed right behind him. They left the door open and Snow Ball and Tiger came in too. Snow Ball jumped up on my desk and started purring. Dillon reached out to pet her head.

"What'd you say about us and . . . " I rolled my eyes toward Dillon and Jennifer, " . . . the incident?"

"Aside from regrets all around, we never got to any basics. The keys were the only substance. They represent our legal permission to get into Harry's office."

"And what about little Harry junior?"

"I can see why they were fighting for custody. Harry junior came in with Judy and quietly worked on his homework. He paid no attention to what we were doing, treating us and our talk for the bullshit it was. Once he went over and climbed into his mother's lap to reassure her. The Moonies can't touch him. He's the only one in that family with his head screwed on right. Jennifer would like him."

"Who would I like?" Jennifer asked, looking up from pulling a piece of string along the floor for Tiger to chase. Her hair was pinned back with her favorite barrettes.

"A boy we were talking about," I said.

"What's his name?"

"You don't know him."

"Well, I just want to know his name, Jay."

And why not? If you talk in front of someone you have to be prepared to let her know who you're talking about.

"The boy's name is Harry Sage. Now you know. Don't bother me, okay? Carol and I are talking."

"Oh, he's my friend," Jennifer said.

I immediately regretted telling her not to bother me as she dropped obediently back onto the floor to play with Tiger.

"Your friend?"

"Yeah, he's in my class at school. And he plays in West Side Little League. The Cougars. But he wasn't in school today."

"At P.S. 75?" I asked.

Jennifer looked at me in disgust. She knew I knew where she went to school.

"Jennifer, maybe you could help us," Carol said, seeing an opening I'd missed.

"How?"

"We're trying to find out something about Harry's mother and father. Did he ever say anything about them to you?"

Jennifer shook her head. "No," she said. Then she said. "Wait a minute. One day he said his mom and dad didn't like each other. He knew my real mom and dad were dead. He asked me what it would be like if his mom and dad were dead too."

Jennifer went over and climbed up into Carol's lap and Carol and I exchanged a look as Carol held onto her tight.

"What did you tell him?" Carol asked softly.

"I said you always get a new dad or mom. Like Jay's my dad and you're sort of my mom, right, Carol?"

Carol hugged her more tightly and gave her a smothering kiss. "I love you, Jennifer."

I turned away from them to hide the tears filling my eyes.

Dillon wasn't allowing for any unshared affection. He jumped down and went running to Carol and began tugging at Jennifer, frowning, his head just reaching the top of Carol's desk.

"I want to sit there!"

Carol and I laughed. Jennifer gave us her smile and Dillon showed his dimples.

Jennifer moved over so that both children were now crowded into Carol's lap. Carol looked very happy.

"Maybe you can help us with your friend, Jennifer," I told her. "We'll have to see. But be real nice to him if you see him. His father did die last night."

"Oh!" she said, wide-eyed. She got off of Carol's lap and came over to put an arm around my neck as she stood beside me, as if to reassure us we were okay.

I gave her my own reassuring hug and then turned her around toward the door.

"Okay, you kids take a walk now and find out if Julia has an afternoon snack for you. I'll be back to see you when Carol and I have finished talking."

They each grabbed a cat and disappeared into the hallway. And Jennifer even remembered to pull the door closed behind her.

I looked at Carol and she looked at me. What was there to say?

▽

8

JUST THEN THE DOOR opened again and Charlene of the Bardot face and Rockette legs looked in on us. She was loaded with bags from Saks Fifth Avenue, Lord & Taylor, and Bloomingdale's.

"Hi, Aunt Carol."

Carol actually grimaced. "Just call me Carol, okay, Charlene?"

Charlene shrugged indifferently. "You got time for me to show you some stuff I bought?"

"Sure, what's life like without time to see the results of a shopping spree. But let's go upstairs. Jay won't be appreciative enough and we don't want to waste this."

I watched them go. Then I sat there letting the events of the morning sink in. I picked up Harry's black book and began to flip through the pages. What a lot of women! And Carol hadn't gotten anything out of a single one of them. I had had the only success with Doni. But we had found her through the answering machine tape, not through the book. In fact, the book number for Doni had proved to be wrong.

I picked out the name Melissa at random and dialed the number. A woman answered and even acknowledged she was Melissa.

"Listen, my name is Jay Jasen. I'm a friend of Harry Sage and—"

"You're a friend of that ol' boy?" she cut in, almost bubbling. Her voice had a Southern drawl to it.

"Sure."

"Then we can get together whenever you want, honey."

This burst of cooperation astonished me. I glanced at my watch.

"How's now?"

"You got it, honey. Just come on by our door. Any friend of Harry's is always good to us."

Melissa's apartment was in a residential building on East 50th Street. The building had a doorman. He was a heavyset black guy with a gray mustache and he gave me a wink and a nod when I told him what apartment I wanted. I went on up and found the door open a crack. I knocked anyway.

"Come in," a woman said. The voice didn't have Melissa's drawl. I pushed open the door as the woman came toward me. She had gray eyes and light blond hair tied back in a French braid and her complexion was very white. Her nose was bobbed perfectly as if a surgeon had done it for her. She was smiling and I saw a gap where a tooth was missing. I noticed because I was trying not to look at what I really saw. She had her blouse unbuttoned almost to her navel and I could see the nipple of one breast if she wasn't careful. And she wasn't.

"You Melissa?" I asked her. But I had hesitated with the surprise and she had already turned to lead me into the living room. My question nearly died in my throat. She wore shorts so short the cheeks of her buns flashed as she walked and she had on high heels.

There was a well-equipped bar on one wall and a stereo against the other with vintage Jefferson Airplane coming from the speakers.

"You're Jay, right?" She had stopped by the bar and turned to face me again.

I nodded. "I'm here to see Melissa."

"Sure. I'm Cheryl. How about a drink while you wait?"

"Yeah, okay, I guess so. Will she be long?"

"What'll ya have?"

"Just a beer."

"Bud?"

"Fine."

She poured it into a tall glass and brought it to where I stood near the door.

"Come and sit down," she said and, after handing me the Budweiser, she took my free arm and led me to a large couch where we sat. There were some cheese things on a coffee table and she had to lean against me to reach them. And she did, grabbing hold of my thigh with her near hand so that the fingers slipped into the sensitive inside and also baring her breasts to me as she leaned forward.

I stood up.

"What's wrong?" she said, wide-eyed.

"Well," I said and I had to look away from her before I changed my mind, "I really want to talk to Melissa."

"What's wrong with me?" She looked hurt. "Melissa said she'd never met you. Some john recommended her to you."

"Some john," I said under my breath, sitting down again. She misunderstood and cuddled up to me.

"I'm sorry," I said, "I'm not a john. A guy I know, Harry Sage, was murdered last night. He had Melissa's phone number. I'm trying to track down a couple of things. I need to talk to Melissa."

Cheryl suddenly got modest and began to button up her blouse. "You a cop?"

"No, no. I had some business with this guy. It's okay."

"Oh," Cheryl said and she stopped buttoning. "Melissa's upstairs with a regular. I'll give her a call. Maybe she'll want to talk to you. Maybe not."

Melissa came in a few moments later. She was a tall, light-skinned Black woman and had on a Spandex outfit that let her nipples stick right out. She'd had her hair done so that it was straight and short, pixielike around her face. Her ruby lipstick was smudged. She glanced at me before checking herself in the mirror and fixing the lipstick. But none of it could hide that she was much older than Cheryl. When she'd finished, she turned toward me. I caught her scent then. The same perfume Doni had worn. And I'd first smelled it in Harry's office.

"Make it quick, would you, honey. You know what I'm saying? I'm on the job and there's this guy waiting for me upstairs."

"I'm looking for some information about Harry Sage. He's dead."

"Dead?"

"Murdered last night over on Riverside Drive."

"Yeah, hey, man, yeah, I saw the thing in the paper."

She looked at the floor. "Yeah, yeah, the poor baby. Oh, shit, I'm sorry for your friend. I liked Harry. I mean, I really *liked* him. You know what I'm saying? He come down around here a lot like about six months back. Yeah, he was in and out of here like we had a revolving door for him." She smiled at me. "We had to give the man the king-size discounts. You know what I'm saying?"

"Why'd he stop coming around?"

"I had to send him away. He was one of those johns wants to get involved with you, you know what I'm saying? He was a lover. I had a big fight with him because he wanted to know my name. My real name, you know what I'm saying? Where I lived. First of all, my old man'd kill him. Second, who needs that kind of shit?"

"What kind of shit?"

"Look, this is a job, right? Like any other job, sometimes you enjoy it, sometimes you don't. Sometimes you want to cry. The man wanted something. He even tried to follow me home a couple of times. You know what I'm saying?"

"Yeah," I said, "I know what you're saying." I stood up and took out a business card. "But please, please call me if you think of any reason Harry might have been murdered. Thanks for your time."

"Sorry about Harry. Nothing happened here to get him murdered."

I started for the door.

"Jay?"

I turned toward them. "Yeah?"

"You're a real good-looking guy. We make men happy. Now that you know us, maybe you'll be back. You got the number. We'd like to see you." Melissa looked at me earnestly from under her pixie haircut. To her left, Cheryl leaned against the bar, smiling, looking more naked than dressed with one breast hanging out and her bare legs.

"I know what you're saying," I said again. "It's an idea with appeal. But sometimes I just want to cry. You know what I'm saying?"

I looked back before I closed the door. Melissa had her eyes closed. Cheryl was watching me.

One thing and another, it was after five o'clock when I returned to the brownstone again. The ninety-pound wildcat stood in the hall, her jacket over her arm.

Julia shook her head, accusing me. She says you can't leave a seven- and three-year-old alone even for a few minutes. And I agree with her. But that doesn't stop her from making her point every time I'm five minutes late.

"He's nearly three and a half and they're not my kids," I said defensively.

"Oh, yes, they are your kids. Ever since your brother and his wife were killed and the kids came here. With kids, it's not like living with some woman or being married. You can't quit and walk away. There's nothing halfway. You understand me, Mr. Jasen?" Her black hair and dark-rimmed glasses accentuated her anger nicely.

"Yes, yes, Julia, I understand." Addressing me as Mr. Jasen was always a sign of deep trouble. Perhaps I'd soon have to tell her what was going on. But for now I opened the door to help her get going. When Julia's getting something off her chest it's best to roll with the punch.

"Jennifer and Dillon need a mother. It's no good for a man to raise two kids. You're responsible for these two little children. You know that, right?"

"Maybe Carol—"

Julia made a noise and a face that interrupted me. "Carol, nothing! You know she's not the woman these kids need. They need a real mother, not Carol!"

I'd said it to deflect her anger onto Carol but now I was afraid I'd made a mistake. If Julia got going on Carol . . . Julia's excellent with the kids. She loves them as much as I do, or Carol or anybody else. She would be willing to take care of the children if I was sent off to prison. But I wanted her skills and not her point of view. Our love for them was the same, but raising them was quite another thing.

But Julia gave it up. Perhaps she had to be somewhere or she sensed, for once, that my heart wasn't in it. "Have a nice weekend, okay, Jay?" she said as she put one foot across the doorstep.

"I'll try, Julia, I'll really try." But I closed the door thinking a nice weekend was not in my hands.

I went on into the office. Jennifer and Dillon were sitting on the floor playing with Lego blocks. They push themselves into the office when Julia leaves and give me an excuse to quit work. And they let Tiger and Snow Ball in too. I tried Frederik again with the same bad luck I'd had all day. Then I sat on the floor and put together boats, trucks, and planes from Lego. Mine were the least creative.

But Harry or no Harry, it was Friday night. I needed a break.

Around six o'clock Carol and Charlene were bouncing some suitcases down the stairs. The kids and I came to the hall door. Charlene came up and gave me a big hug.

"Good-bye, Jay. I got a place with a friend today. Aunt Carol —I mean Carol—was really nice to me. I'll see you guys for, you know, Sunday dinner and stuff."

"Anything you need, you call," I said.

She pushed on out the front door and Carol followed her.

Carol surprised me by coming back to the office. She keeps Friday night to herself and, in spite of the crisis, I just assumed she would as usual.

"So Charlene is gone," I said.

Carol nodded. "I hope she'll be okay."

"Kids have to make their own way when they grow up."

Carol looked at me and she didn't look too happy. "I have to have a drink, Jay. Am I mixing one for you, too?"

I nodded. She dug out the Johnny Walker and went to the kitchen. In a few minutes she was back with two tall scotch and waters for us and apple juice for the children, all balanced on a wooden cheese board with cheese and crackers.

The three of us got up and gathered around the cheese board. Then Carol sat on the recliner and I got the couch while Dillon and Jennifer went back to the floor.

"I know how you can get hold of Frederik," Carol said.

"Me too," I replied without enthusiasm. I didn't feel like spending the night drinking. And who knew? Maybe the fat woman witness was touring the local bars with the cops? I went on, "Just get to the Silver Bar Café after ten tonight. Frederik would never miss a Friday."

I swear neither of us said a word again for five minutes.

"Better that way than no way," Carol said.

"Okay," I said, "I'll do it. But if I do, let's go have dinner somewhere first."

"Okay," Carol said, surprising me.

"I wanna go too." Dillon jumped to his feet and ran to get his jacket. You think the kids aren't tuned in and suddenly you say something and they are right smack in your face with it. Jennifer, wiser, continued to play.

"Can we go too, Jay?" she asked.

"Unless I can get Meagan over," I said. Meagan, the teenage baby-sitter who lives down the block, is their favorite person in the world. She lets them do anything they want. I called and Meagan said she'd be over in five minutes.

"Meagan's coming," I told Dillon when he reappeared with his jacket on.

"Meagan's coming," he shouted with joy. He tore off the jacket and dumped it on the floor. "Meagan's coming to my house," he told his sister, who was designing a Lego apartment house.

"I know," she said as if to tell me not to repeat myself, but she was smiling too.

While Carol went upstairs to change, I took frozen fish sticks out of the freezer and got them into the microwave. Meagan arrived just as Carol came back. She's tall, over six feet, with long brown hair and a great full-faced smile which, because she's a teenager, is nearly impossible to get from her.

"We're having dinner at the Balcony Restaurant up at 106th and Broadway," I told Meagan, looking to Carol, who nodded that the choice was fine with her. "After that, I'll be at the Silver Bar Café, okay?"

Meagan said she understood.

We left them there alone.

▽

9

OUTSIDE WE HAD A beautiful spring night. We walked up West End Avenue instead of Broadway, opting for the residential feeling.

"Well, some women in the book are prostitutes," I said.

She stopped to look me in the face. I told her about Melissa and about going over there.

Carol laughed. "I guess I got pretty mad at the women I called. I admit they were smart not to open up to a stranger."

"I feel dumb that I didn't call Bruce Scarf that night at Harry's right after I'd called 911," I told her.

At the Balcony, the maître d' sat us at the table for four along the Broadway rail of the outside cafe. We could sit and watch the crowd pass.

We ordered another round of drinks and dinner, Carol the almond chicken and me the stuffed bluefish. She had white wine but I nursed my scotch so I'd have some memory later, at the Silver Bar Café.

While I was eating, I felt a tug at my sleeve. I turned and found myself looking up at a woman of my age leaning in from the sidewalk. She wore no jewelry and had on a plain brown sweater and skirt. She held out a pound box of chocolates. I recognized her scent. Had she been in Harry's office the night before?

"Support our program for children. Please buy one box."

Startled, I held up my hand and waved her off. And she moved on to the next table just as Carol looked up at her.

"Judy!" Carol said.

The woman glanced back at Carol. She waved her hand so minimally that I wasn't sure she had reacted. Then she moved on.

"That's Harry's wife, Judy Sage." Carol looked up and down at the people on Broadway. "Looks like she's alone."

Carol stood up and leaned out over the sidewalk.

"Judy," she called. Judy looked back and Carol gave an emphatic wave for her to come over. This time she came back to us. Although she wasn't wearing her sexuality like Melissa or Doni, Judy was attractive. She would have looked like a model rather than gaunt if it weren't for the glassy Moonie smile and the dark circles under her clear blue eyes. Her dark brown hair was pulled back into a pony tail. And she was wearing that scent.

"Hello," she said to Carol, "I didn't think I'd be seeing you again so soon. You must live around here."

"Yes, nearby. Look, this is Harry's partner, Jay Jasen." Carol gestured to me.

"Oh, hello," Judy said brightly. "You and Carol are going to buy Harry's business, right?"

"Yes, we hope to." I stole a sharp look at Carol.

"Won't you come and sit with us?" Carol asked.

Judy continued to smile, but she shrank back from us as if we were evil.

"I can't. I have to sell this stuff. Our Church needs the money to do good things for children all over the world." She pulled a second box of chocolates from her bag and held the two boxes up. "Maybe you could each buy one and help us with our work. We're going to save the world."

The brilliance of her smile said she wasn't attempting irony.

"We're trying to figure out why Harry was killed," I said, annoyed. "Stop for a moment and see if you can help us."

She shrank back from us again. "I can't," she said. Then she was asking the next table—for a second time—to buy her chocolates before either of us could blink. We'd lost our chance.

"Pardon me," Carol said. She left me and went over to where Judy was working and I could see them talking. Judy came back with her. I had a chair pulled out when they got to the table.

"We don't drink," she said when I offered. But Carol insisted on ordering and Judy got a Diet Coke and a bowl of chili.

"Judy's a member of the Unification Church," Carol told me as if I didn't know.

"I'm sorry about this," Judy said in a moment of self-recognition and she patted the bag of candy she had placed on one corner of the table. "I know other people think we're silly but it's a way to acquire some humility."

"We have a common problem," Carol said. "Neither Jay nor I know much about Harry. What did he do that caused him to be murdered?"

Judy was already shaking her head. "I didn't ever want to see him again. Harry junior was my only contact. I have a new family now." Judy beamed at us with her goddamned Moonie smile.

The waitress interrupted us with Judy's chili and Diet Coke. Judy dug into it as if she hadn't eaten for a week.

"It's nice you have a new family," Carol said as Judy ate. "Jay has an adopted daughter named Jennifer who is a friend of Harry junior's at P.S. 75." Carol stopped and looked puzzled. "I thought the Unification Church had schools?"

For the first time Judy looked disturbed and her smile disappeared.

"Yes," she said simply, and then she was quiet but seemed to be working on something, so Carol and I kept our mouths shut. "Harry wouldn't let me put little Harry into the

Church's school. That's why Harry junior is still at P.S. 75. Now his father's dead, I can put him in the Church school. But I think he should finish the year at P.S. 75." She beamed at us again.

"But I understood Reverend Moon wanted you to leave your child with your former life mate rather than bring him into the Church?" Carol went on. She was hitting the weak point. Judy's smile vanished again.

"I don't understand it," Judy said. "Everything else is clear. But I don't think our Father meant for us to give up our children. Little Harry is staying with me." Judy did not go back to smiling.

"My life was a mess before I found the Church." Judy's voice rose as she got into it. "Harry had other women. He always had to screw other women. I couldn't stand him doing that to his son." She began to shout. "It wasn't once. It was his way of life. He wanted to get his penis into every woman in the world. We even had to take shots for syphilis!"

Judy had gotten quite loud, talking of Harry. First, a guy at the next table turned and then we were on stage for everybody.

Carol put a hand on Judy's arm. "Go easy now. Harry's dead."

"I'm sorry," Judy said quietly. She stood up at the table looking at us and at the people watching us. Her chili bowl was empty. "You see what I mean. I haven't gone crazy like that in a month." She stopped looking at us and began to empty her bag of chocolates on the chair.

"Jay," Carol said, "give Judy a check for seventy dollars for the Unification Church."

"The chocolate . . . " I began awkwardly.

"Judy said she could only stop if she sold her chocolate. I promised we'd buy."

I knew when to keep my mouth shut. I wrote the check and handed it to Judy not even worrying about what percent was tax deductible.

"Thank you," Judy said. But she hadn't found the Moonie

smile again, and with the circles under her eyes on her thin face, she looked very sick. "The Church has helped me find purpose in life. And to forget the way Harry treated me. Maybe I don't agree a hundred percent with everything, like the way the children are educated, but most of it is good."

She turned to leave us.

"Just a minute," Carol said, "I'll walk out with you."

I looked up at Carol as she rose, but her eyes were on Judy. Then she turned to me.

"I'll see you in the morning," she said. I nodded to her and they were gone.

"Hey, I think you're the guy I'm looking for."

I hadn't seen her coming. Her eyes were silver. Yes, silver. It must have been the dim light and some trick of her iris pigment. But she caught me with the eyes and startled me. I pretended my jumping up was an act of politeness.

Who was she?

I looked at the rest of her to get away from the eyes. She had dark hair cut short. Her body was hidden under a man's white linen jacket that was too large but she wore it stylishly with the sleeves turned back at the cuffs. She had diamond studs in her ears, a Cartier watch on her left wrist, and a single gold chain around her neck.

"Aren't you Jay Jasen?"

"Yes," I stumbled over the simple word. "I'm Jay Jasen."

"I'm Jackie. Jackie McKensie."

She took off the coat and tossed it onto an empty chair as she dropped into another. Under it she had on a sleeveless peach-colored silk blouse that her breasts filled without stretching anything.

I carefully took my own seat again. As I did, I shifted my focus from her blouse back to her eyes. Her own gaze was now directed at people on Broadway so I didn't feel embarrassed by seeing her eyes again. She licked her lips with the tip of her tongue.

No one should be handicapped by being too beautiful,

especially in the full sexual way of Jackie: a finely sculptured face but with a thin nose that flared at the nostrils, and full lips. And a little twist upward at the corner of her mouth that brought the word *yes* into my mind involuntarily. I found it impossible to sit there and not continually think about how beautiful she was. I had to look away.

She turned to me, trying to smile, nervous, showing her teeth. They were small and animal-like, something not so beautiful as the rest of her. She closed her mouth as if she knew.

Her showing up threw me a curve for a second reason too. How could a stranger find me so easily? I didn't like it with Harry hanging over my head. I glanced around to see if anyone was watching us. Not that I could spot anyone, except for several men, including the guy at the next table who had been disturbed by Judy's shouting. But hell, their eyes were on Jackie, not me.

"Do you mind that I've come to see you?" She took out a cigarette as she spoke and tapped it a couple of times on the table before lighting it.

"Who are you," I asked, "and how do you know who I am?"

She took a drag on the cigarette and smiled again, a thin smile, not so nervous this time, as if she were conscious of the teeth and how not to show them.

"It's easy enough to figure out. You see, I was Harry Sage's mistress."

My chin hit my knees. Harry involved with a woman so incredibly beautiful? She made Doni or Judy look like nothing. I don't think she noticed because she turned to listen to the waitress. Jackie pointed to my drink and asked for a double. I nodded reflexively when the waitress looked at me.

Why would she be with Harry? What attracted her to him? And if Harry had Jackie as his mistress, Doni as his lover, and Judy as his wife, how did he have any energy for other women? Why would he want other women? I looked at Jackie again and gulped.

"Today," she went on, "I called Harry's office. No one was there. So I called Fran at home. She told me Harry was dead, murdered. She had spoken to you. She said you were his partner or something. Well, you know how Fran is. Spills the beans, so to speak. She gave me your number. It was earlier tonight. I reached a girl. She said you'd be here."

It did make me nervous that anyone could be tracking me down. I took another look around and again saw nothing but the men watching Jackie.

"But this place is crowded. And you've never seen me before."

"Yeah," she said, giving me a grim look. "But only one was married to Harry. When I saw Judy I held back until she left. She's the last human being I wanted to see. And the man she was talking to must be Jay Jasen, right?"

It was a clever piece of reasoning. I'd been playing with the stem of my water glass to avoid her eyes. The waitress placed our drinks on the table. Then I looked right at her.

"You still have to tell me why you went to all that trouble."

Jackie looked away from me, took a drink of her scotch and sagged back into her chair as if uncertain, distant, punching out the cigarette in an ashtray.

"Harry," she said, but she only said the name, not like a response to me, but a statement of everything.

I waited but she seemed stuck. "Harry?" I repeated.

"What?" She looked at me as if she had just seen me there. "Oh, nothing."

Without warning she put her hands up to her face and sobbed loudly, shaking convulsively.

The guy at the next table who had first taken in Judy now turned around to see Jackie fully. He must have begun to wonder what this parade of distressed women was doing at my table. Even for New York it was beginning to look a little bizarre. I smiled at him and he looked away.

"I just can't believe it," Jackie sobbed. "Just last night."

She leaned forward into her hands and cried loudly. Now people passing on Broadway looked in at us. The guy next to us appeared ready to get up. I noticed he was a pretty big guy.

I reached out and gripped her by the forearm. She seemed really upset.

"It's going to be okay," I said.

She jerked her arm away, but then stopped crying. She lifted her head and looked at me straight on. Her eyes were beautiful and they made me want to put my arms around her.

"No, it's not going to be okay," she said. "What happened? What happened to Harry?"

Now that I had gotten over the surprise of her arrival I was reeling from the circumstances of Harry's life. Jackie was the second lover to come forward in the day since his murder. Two, plus a wife and a prostitute who knew him and said he'd tried to get intimate. Carol had been right. The black book must be filled with every woman he had ever known. Maybe it was a scorecard. And we had just scratched the surface. But now I knew a possible motive: jealousy.

But what could a jealous lover have to do with my having a partnership with Harry? What the hell was going on anyway?

"Did you kill Harry?"

Okay, it was a blunt question. But I was on my own roller coaster even if I wasn't exactly sobbing into my hands. The surprise question might cause her to slip up.

The grimace on her face was real. I couldn't tell whether the question or my style determined it. She rose to her feet, the tears streaming down her face.

"I shouldn't have come," she said in a voice I nearly couldn't hear.

I stood beside her and put an arm around her shoulders and gently urged her back down. It took my breath away to touch her. She didn't resist me. Close to her I recognized the same perfume that had wafted through Harry's office. That was four for four.

"I'm sorry," was all I could think to say.

"Why is all this happening?" She shook her head as if to clear her emotions.

"I don't know. I don't know anything."

We sat silent. My blunt question had thrown us both into shock.

I looked into her eyes. She returned my gaze without flinching. And she spoke first.

"What can I do?" It struck me that I should have asked her that question. And did she mean, what should she do herself? Or what should she do to help me? There was no reason she should help me. There was no way she could know that I needed help desperately. And I wasn't about to talk about the partnership in the way that had almost caused Doni to walk away from me.

But I asked her, "Can you think of any reason Harry should be dead?"

Jackie shook her head slowly. "He liked jazz. He liked to dance."

I thought she was going to break down again. She didn't.

"I was his mistress and Harry was my lover. You know what it's like when your lover dies?"

She paused but I wasn't about to tell her about dogs and lovers.

She went on. "You have no right to anything. You want me to talk to his estranged wife? His helpful secretary?" Anger was replacing sorrow. "Or to his male business partner who I'd never even met? You might tell me to go fly a kite and there's not a goddamned thing I could do." Her eyes flashed at me. "But my looks aren't half bad, are they? And I trusted you as a man to take pity on me. That's why I had to be here. For you to see me and give me everything I wanted. Something no rival woman with Harry would ever give me."

She stopped suddenly and her mouth made a firm, tight line and she took me all in. She had successfully turned it around.

"What can I do to help?" I asked her and then I had to stare down into the tabletop, waiting.

She reached across and grabbed my hand. My heart stopped.

"Come on," she said, "let's get out of here."

She polished off the double scotch, grabbed her white linen jacket, and went to recompose herself while I settled the check. It gave me a chance to think.

The evening had taken an unexpected turn. Carol and I had intended a quiet dinner; instead, we couldn't get through dinner without two of Harry's women popping up like storybook cutouts. Now Carol was off chasing down crazy Judy, a Moonie. And I had been sought out by one of Harry's million lovers. How could I proceed without offending Jackie? Harry was dead. She was beautiful. I was an unattached male. How could I even think of sex and involvement at a time like this? She wasn't here looking for a new lover.

She came back and I looked at her. She was really something. She looked into my eyes and I could see she was puzzled. But we went, and I left Judy's chocolates behind, sitting on the chair.

We walked up Broadway, side by side. "I want to know something about Harry," she said.

"Listen, anything I can do for you," I said again. "But I want to check in the Silver Bar for a friend. Then we can talk."

Jackie kept her thoughts to herself until we were waiting for the light to cross 110th.

"Harry and I used to go to the Silver Bar," she said. "It was always a final call after the theater or a film. Yes, a Friday night like this. Sometimes the band is very good."

We became quiet again as we crossed the street.

"Other times we'd spend the whole night at the West End jazz room just listening and watching the people."

We went into the Silver Bar.

"Buy me a drink," Jackie said. "It would help me to have a drink here."

"A table or the bar?"

"The bar for old times' sake."

She hung up the white jacket while I pushed ahead of her

into the bar making a small place to stand together. It was the same spot as the week before. The last time I'd seen Harry alive. He'd stood right there a few inches from where Jackie was now.

"Hi, Jimmy," Jackie said to the bartender. "You heard about Harry, right?"

Jimmy was a big guy who worked out. He leaned over the bar to her. "Yeah. I'm real sorry for you and him." He shook his head in disbelief. "You never know, do ya."

She shook her head with him. "I needed to stop for some memories." Her eyes filled up with tears and I couldn't help looking down into them.

Jimmy shook his head again and was called away, but not before Jackie ordered double scotches for both of us. "It's on us," he said when he brought them back.

Jackie raised her glass to mine. "In remembrance of Harry," she said. We touched glasses and I looked again into her eyes as we drank. My God, it was something. The crowd forced us close and I couldn't stand it. There was a band this Friday and it was doing old rock music well, stimulated by Columbia and Barnard students.

"It feels right being here," she said. "Harry liked this place."

"This is the last place I saw Harry alive, only a week ago tonight."

"You see your friend?"

I took a quick look around. Frederik wasn't there. I took another look around for Chinless but with no luck.

I shook my head for her. "He's not here."

"Who is it?"

"A guy named Frederik. You ever meet him? They call him Flash in here because he hustles the bowling machine."

She shook her head. "I don't think so. Maybe if I see him . . . "

"Well, he's not here now."

The band struck up with their version of "Great Balls of Fire" and it put the room into motion.

"Come on," Jackie said, "let's dance. You can't object to dancing. It's never depressing and it stops a hangover. And it will do me good, too, like a jazz band on a tailgate."

I gave her a funny look but she smiled and said, "This is like a wake. Haven't you ever been to a wake?" She pulled on my arm and we moved out onto the small dance floor crowded with students. And we danced. And she was very, very good. People watched her because she was good and she quickly made her own space. Men watched her because they had to. I had to. I couldn't get away from wanting her. Who was Harry to me? I never liked him when he was alive.

In the middle of dancing with her I looked up—really looking at nothing—and saw Chinless George standing at the bar. Chinless was watching me, not Jackie. He had his black hair slicked back and a funny smile cut across his face showing a missing tooth. His eyes made contact with mine. He nodded quickly and disappeared into the crowd at the bar. I shifted my own gaze to Jackie again and watched her dance.

At the end she grabbed my hand and kissed me on the cheek.

"I can see why Harry liked to bring you here. You really dance, don't you?"

Still holding her hand I looked back to the bar. Chinless had disappeared. She saw my expression change. "Damn," I said.

"What's the matter?" She looked up at me and put an arm around my waist.

"Nothing," I said, but I pulled away, almost peeling myself off her. She looked hurt but I left her there and pushed my way through the crowd toward the bar where Chinless had been standing.

"Jimmy," I called. He looked over and waved, filling a pitcher of draft.

"What's your pleasure, Jay?" he shouted.

"You seen Chinless?"

He looked up and down the bar. "Jeez, he was right here.

Maybe he went down to the men's room."

Jackie had pushed in alongside. "What's up, Jay? What's wrong with you?"

"Just wait a second and I'll tell you." I ran down to the basement men's room but no dice. Chinless was gone. When I came back, Jackie grabbed my hand.

"Hey, what's up?"

I looked at her. She looked at me, first into one eye and then into the other as if she wanted to see something there.

"There was a man at the bar, Chinless George. He was with me and Harry last Friday night." She was still looking into my eyes. Chinless George seemed to matter less and less. "I want to ask him if he talked to Harry. But he's gone." She moved in closer and put an arm around me so we were hugging one another. I didn't really give a damn about Chinless.

"Let's move on," Jackie said. She grabbed the white jacket and we walked out onto Broadway holding hands. At her insistence, we looked into Cannon's, Marlin's, Jack's Tavern, and even the Abbey before we ended up in front of the West End. But no luck. George had dropped out of sight. And Frederik wasn't around. The cool night air washed over us and Jackie stood close.

"Well," I said, "I came up here to talk to two guys about Harry. One wasn't at home and the other got away. But I did get to meet you."

Jackie smiled at me, her thin smile. "I'm glad I found you for tonight," she said. "I was going crazy over Harry. You helped me out."

I could almost look her in the eyes without thinking about wanting her.

"Look," she said, pointing to the poster in the window, "it's the Caliph Quintet of Jazz tonight. They play good stuff. Take me into the jazz room. After a set, maybe those guys you're looking for will show up."

She smiled up at me, even letting the teeth show this time, and tugged at one arm. There was no reason to refuse.

So Jackie and I ended up sitting in the jazz room at the West End listening to the Caliph Quintet. And she was right. They were very, very good.

"Harry liked jazz a lot," Jackie told me after the first piece.

We had ordered drinks again, but we hadn't finished those at the Silver Bar and I was feeling good but not out of control.

"He loved to come here," she went on, "and listen through a couple of sets and watch the people."

We were sitting next to each other at a small table facing the jazz players. It was easier not having to look directly at her.

"It's great music," I said.

The Caliphs' adaptation of "Grazing in the Grass" kept us quiet; we sipped our drinks and listened. Jackie took out a cigarette and tapped it on the table and lit it.

When they finished the set, Abdullah, the quintet's leader, made his way over to Jackie. He was a big, balding black man with gray hair and a white mustache who stooped slightly as though blowing on his sax even when he wasn't, as though always immersed in his music. Jackie was pulling out another cigarette as he came up and he took out a lighter and lit it for her.

His voice sounded like he had a mouth full of gravel. "We saw what happened to your old man. We were real sorry."

"Thank you, Abdullah," Jackie said. "This is a friend of Harry's. Jay Jasen."

Abdullah nodded to me.

"We came here tonight because Harry would have come. It's a little memory of good things together," she went on.

"This next piece is for him—and you," Abdullah told her, "two good people. We'll all miss him."

Jackie's eyes glistened with tears. She thanked him again and he made his way back to the quintet.

The Caliphs did a cover of "St. James Infirmary" that seemed to roll off their instruments, a tribute Jackie could hold on to forever. And Abdullah sang the last verse for her, his gravel-filled baritone giving it an unforgettable sense:

Let 'im go, let 'im go, God bless 'im,
(Amen)
Wherever he may be.
(Yeah, man)
He'll search this whole world over,
(Tell it, sing it out)
And never find another woman like her.
(Yeah, right, nobody)

Jackie was crying as he sang, but it was a happy crying with smiles, and she hugged my arm.

Maybe Harry had been a lot better guy than I had given him credit for.

Jackie and I applauded vigorously as did everyone, and we stood too, Jackie shouting "Bravo." Abdullah and the Caliphs bowed toward her three times.

"I'm sure Harry loved it," she called.

"Thank you," Abdullah called back and blew her a kiss. Then he turned and the Caliphs started their next piece.

We sat back down and Jackie moved up close to me so that her arm was intertwined with mine and she was snuggled loosely against my side. She squeezed my hand.

"This and stopping at the Silver Bar were nice ways to remember Harry."

"I'm glad it turned out this way."

Jackie took a drag on her cigarette. Then she looked me in the eyes close up again with that way she had of looking in one eye and then the other so I felt like I just wanted to talk with my eyes for the rest of my life.

"Tell me something I don't know about Harry," she said. "Something nice."

That was a hard question for me. I was only now finding out about Harry's good side myself. Yet I didn't want to disappoint her.

"He really loved his kid," I said. "You know his wife split from him and joined the Moonies."

She nodded, looking into my eyes without blinking.

"Well, Harry was doing everything he could to gain custody. There was no way he was going to let the Moonies take over his kid. He made sure Harry junior stayed in a good public school and even had him in a West Side Little League team to keep his life normal."

Her eyes were glistening again. "That was nice about him—his love for his kid." She looked like someone I wanted to hold forever.

"You were his business partner, right?" she went on. "Was he okay as a business partner?"

She startled me with the question.

"What did he say about our partnership?" I asked her, naturally, without thinking it was a question I would have planned to ask her.

She just shrugged. "Nothing. He just said you'd really be a good partner for him. You knew what you were doing." She stopped. "Why did you ask me that?"

"No reason."

"What was it like then, being his partner?"

"Well, to tell you the truth, we had just started out. There's not much I can tell you. It appeared we were going to make money—at least Harry thought so. But now I don't know what will happen."

"What were you doing and was Harry good at it?"

She looked at me, one eye and then the other, searching.

I smiled and tried to appear knowledgeable, remembering Harry's letterhead as the only tip I had: Jasen & Sage, Tax Investigations. I was safe enough since I knew nothing myself.

"We did tax investigations. You know, finding where the money was hidden kind of thing. It's hard to say how we worked together—the work was so much each of us doing his own project."

I paused, not telling her I had carried out zero investigations and didn't know what the hell Harry had in mind.

I looked at her face as she watched the Caliphs start another piece. I couldn't stop myself from thinking again of that face on the pillow beside me. She drew on her cigarette and blew the smoke out.

"Sounds a little strange," she said. She looked at me sharply. "What did you two have that could kill you?"

I shrugged because there was nothing else I could do. "I can't tell you."

"You can't or you won't?" she said.

"There's nothing to tell." I wasn't certain I could get her to believe me.

She stubbed out the cigarette. "He was so private about his business," she said. "I never had any idea what he had going except for tax returns. He never told me about you."

"He didn't tell anybody very much."

The set ended and Jackie went up to thank Abdullah and the Caliphs while I settled the check. Then we were out on Broadway again.

"You should go home," I said.

Jackie looked up at me with her eyes. They seemed silver again in the dim light of Broadway. I wanted to believe she wanted me as much as I wanted her. But it was only a day since Harry had been murdered. Even if her thoughts were also on us going home together, it couldn't be a good idea—not this night. We'd be haunted by Harry.

She took my arm and we walked down 114th Street to her building on Riverside Drive. She held on just as tightly as I wished she would. I saw her into the elevator and left her there. Neither of us had said a word and then she looked into my eyes, into one and then the other. She squeezed my hand and let go. The elevator door closed.

▽

10

THE ENTRANCE TO JACKIE'S building opens onto 114th. The air seemed crisper, cooler. Rather than turn up to Broadway, I went down to Riverside Drive and walked south toward 110th. At 112th I turned the corner and ran into a crowd that had spilled out from a party onto the sidewalk making noise and leaving no room to pass. I turned to go around and I ran straight into Chinless George coming around the corner.

"Chinless," I said, surprised, grabbing his arm because he was so intent and going so fast he hadn't recognized me. His mouth was in a straight line across the bottom of his face and his slicked-back hair was out of place here and there. He had a way of looking out of the corners of his dark eyes when he talked that made me think of a gypsy.

He pulled up and looked at me like that. First, it was to see who I was, and second, in genuine surprise, examining me like some unsuspecting fresh victim for a bowling game.

"I was just looking for you," I said.

"You was looking for me?" he said, an edge of additional surprise in his voice.

"Yeah, that night—last Friday—after I left you bowling with Harry and Flash, I went across the street for some food.

When I came out you guys were flagging a cab. What happened? Where did you go?"

Chinless looked over my shoulder at the loud crowd.

"Nuttin' happened," he said. He looked at me out of the corner of his eyes again. "What's up? He owe you some money?"

"He's dead."

Chinless let out a low whistle.

"Murdered." I wanted to shake him up. "Up the street here on Riverside Drive. They knifed him until he died."

I got Chinless to roll his eyes.

"Nuttin' happened," he said again. "We took off for another bowling machine downtown. Me and Flash, we busted him and we was flush. We went looking for some fresh money."

"What'd Harry say he was doing?"

Now he really stopped and thought as though I'd tossed him the sixty-four-thousand dollar question, looking around as if about to make some illegal proposition.

"What the fuck was he doing, anyway?" Chinless asked me in answer.

"Part of it was taxes," I said. "He had a tax business. Like me."

Chinless smiled showing his missing tooth. "If he's dead, I guess it don't hurt to tell you."

He shuffled a step away. I swallowed hard.

"He kept playing double or nuttin' until he was in over his head. But he paid me and Flash off. Get this. He paid us off with coke." He stopped and his mouth opened into what passed for a smile and then he said, "and he paid us off with girls." George laughed out loud.

"Coke!" I said. "And women!"

Chinless frowned and looked around. "Keep your voice down, would ya, Jay?" he advised me. "Yeah, coke. He bragged that he kept the local jazz bands in snow."

I stood there, speechless.

"Look, Jay, I gotta get going," Chinless said.

"You headed to the Silver Bar?"

Chinless nodded and I tagged along with him. The crowd had thinned out with the arrival of a police car.

Visions of prison sentences danced through my head. Coke! Women! What kind of partnership had Harry brought me into? Why had I signed the partnership agreement and allowed Carol to give a copy to Judy's Moonie advisers? Did Jackie know anything about this? Did Doni? Did Melissa or Judy? Did Fran? How many people did?

But from what I'd seen, Harry kept all the parts of his life so separate that it was just dumb luck to find Chinless George who'd been there when Harry was drunk and losing. And Harry had talked and acted.

We were crossing Broadway before I found myself secure enough to ask Chinless more.

"Frederik—Flash—with you the whole time?"

"Flash come over with us to the girls. But, ya know, Flash's funny. He don't like no drug but alcohol. He'd have a shot of Wild Turkey before he'd do a line of coke. Ya know what I mean? And I tell you this was royal coke. He took a girl, though. He took her right home. She was good-looking, too. A young blonde with big tits and a tight-looking ass. Wish I'd 'a gotten her first." Chinless shook his head at the woman he'd missed.

I said nothing. I didn't think there was anything else that George could tell me. And I was not about to confide my problems to him. So we were quiet walking down the block to the Silver Bar Café.

"I hope some of the students have cleared off," George muttered as we pushed in. But he was out of luck. The Silver Bar was crowded.

I left Chinless and threaded my way into the bar, waving for Jimmy. He saw me and came over.

"You seen Flash?" I asked.

"I don't think I seen him tonight," Jimmy said. "But I could'a missed him." He started to turn away and then he clicked his fingers and pointed at me.

"You got a phone call after you'd left."

"I did? Here? Who'd call me here?"

"I don't know who it was. A girl. Said if you came back to tell you, you was robbed at home."

"What!" I shouted. People at the bar turned to see why I was shouting. Someone down the bar called for Jimmy. He shrugged his shoulders.

"Yeah, that was it. There was a break-in. You better go home." He moved off down the bar.

I pushed my way out through the crowd. Chinless stood near the door with a drink looking smug. Frederik was next to him, his black beard looking more shot through with gray than when last I'd seen him.

"Mr. Jasen," Frederik called to me, "don't leave yet. I'm getting a drink and we'll be bowling for dollars."

I rushed past him, saying nothing. Outside I flagged a cab and jumped in.

Two police cars sat, red lights flashing, in front of the brownstone. The cab driver couldn't find change for my five. I went running up the steps without it. A glass panel of the foyer door was smashed and scattered over the foyer and lobby. The door to my apartment hung at a crazy angle opened hinge-side, the door pivoting on the lock.

Two cops stood just inside the door.

"The children! Where are they?" I shouted.

The bigger one, with red hair and a mustache, put a finger up to his lips.

"You Jay Jasen?"

"Yes, yes." I still shouted.

He held his finger up again. "Keep it quiet. Your kids are asleep."

I felt a rush of relief. I went past them into the office. Meagan sat calmly talking to a plainclothes policeman with a duty book in his hand. I knew the guy, a short, squat fireplug of a man, Detective Garner. He'd covered the robbery at my brother's apartment and knew Scarf.

"Hi, Jay," Meagan said brightly. And around her on the floor were the financial guts of several hundred tax clients.

I grabbed her and gave her a hug for being there.

"Meagan, what happened?"

"Oh," Meagan said in a matter-of-fact tone, "a big man with a sledgehammer and chisel busted his way in. He didn't even ring the bell."

"What did you do?"

"I took Jennifer and Dillon into your bedroom, locked the door, and called the police. He didn't bother us. Just came straight through into your office and trashed your files. He left real quick. Like five minutes after he'd got here. Someone tooted a horn out front and he took off."

"When did it happen?"

"Over an hour ago. I had to wake up Jennifer while he was busting down the door. But I could carry Dillon. He slept through the whole thing."

"Meagan, you're wonderful," I said, and I gave her a big hug again. Then I remembered Carol. "Why isn't Carol here?"

Meagan shook her head. "I don't think Carol's home yet. I thought she was with you."

Detective Garner was standing and watching me. "What do you think they were after, Mr. Jasen?"

I took my time, looking around me at the mess of tax returns. I went over in my mind giving up the whole charade and telling him the truth. But there was too much I knew nothing about. Coke? Women? What did I think they were after?

"I don't know." It wasn't hard to look perplexed.

"You don't know?"

"No idea."

He gestured toward the mess on the floor. "Looks like they wanted something besides money."

"Maybe after I sort it out, I'll know what's been taken and it will all fit together."

Garner flipped closed his duty book and looked me right

in the eye. "It's a little bizarre, you know. This guy takes the time and effort to bust in with a sledge and chisel. And he's ready to look fast and leave. And you don't know what it's about."

I shook my head again but had the feeling he was reading my mind.

"I'll give you a call when I come on duty tomorrow. See what you can think of by then."

What would I think of? That I was a drug kingpin or something? I walked him to the door expecting the walls to scream out the truth. The other two cops joined him and they stepped outside. Then Garner turned one more time.

"We'll have a patrol car keep an eye on your door tonight. But get a board and nail it up over the broken glass. That should keep you secure for the night."

The words "secure for the night" echoed through my head. I nodded dumbly. Meagan left with them, and the three cops and I watched until she had entered her building down the block. Garner and the cops got into the cars and drove away. I stumbled back into the apartment and found some plywood, a hammer, and nails.

Would the guy with the sledge come back? With a gun? I pounded the nails through the plywood into the foyer door frame to cover the busted-out windows, oblivious to the damage the nails might be causing. He had broken through the window and then reached in and opened the street door. But there was no way I could fix my apartment door, which he'd busted right off the hinge side. I had Harry's gun, didn't I? Maybe not. I ran into the office and looked into the drawer. The revolver was there on top of the black book. The thief had gone only for the tax files, not for my desk. I stuck the gun into my belt. But what did I know about fighting? Was I willing to blow someone's face away even if he was a murderer? I felt panic surging up in my blood, the panic a rabbit must feel at night when the weasel is digging down into his warren.

Dillon doesn't wake up easily. I shook him too hard. He

sat up, wet his pants, and began to bawl. Jennifer was awakened by all the commotion and looked down at us from her bunk.

"What's the matter, Dad?"

I was glad she called me Dad right then. It helped settle me down.

"Get dressed, Jennifer. We're getting an early start on our weekend house."

Dillon stood by his bed rubbing his eyes. I stripped off his wet pajamas and got him into a fresh dry pair for sleep in the car. I scooped him up and took Jennifer by the hand. He remembered his glasses for me. Once outside, I looked both ways suspiciously. Luckily, no innocent bystander stumbled upon this wild-eyed father bear with his cubs. I was ready to gun people down.

We had to walk to Broadway to find a cab. One pulled up, but the driver took a look at me and sped away.

I cursed when a second one did the same.

"Jay," Jennifer said, "I think the gun is scaring them."

She pointed and I saw that Harry's revolver in my belt was visible to the cab drivers. I stuck it out of sight under my shirt.

But before I had time to wave at another cab, Jennifer was pulling at my hand.

"Wait a second, Jay," she said, "aren't you forgetting about Little League tomorrow?"

Jennifer and Dillon had not been swept up in my panic. Now her simple day-to-day factual expression of what was supposed to happen made me drop my flagging hand.

"I'm supposed to get a chance to play first base," she went on. She was awake now and was seeing her chance to make the big time in Little League slipping away. "Why do we have to go this weekend? You promised me we could stay in town for all the Little League games." She actually began to pout. "It's not fair."

And she had me. Why rush off to our country house in the middle of the night? I had the gun. We could secure ourselves in the apartment. The police would be checking up frequently at our door. And Jennifer could play first base for the Zebras in the morning.

"Come on," I said to Jennifer sheepishly. "Let's go home."

"Thanks, Dad," Jennifer had the presence of mind to say.

Dillon, asleep, stayed cuddled up in my arms until I put him back into the bunk bed.

Jennifer stayed awake to help me push some furniture up against the apartment door after I'd propped it up in place and used wedges to temporarily secure it.

At the end she stood in the hallway with her hands on her hips. "Why did that guy come into our apartment? Is there something going on I don't know about?"

I watched her standing there looking so adult and I laughed. "I love you, Jennifer." But she wasn't letting me brush her off.

"Is he going to come back?"

"I don't think so. If he does, we're ready for him, right?" She nodded and I gave her a big hug and sent her to bed. Then I peeked out the front window and saw a police car stationed by the nearest fire hydrant. It made me feel better even though I was the guy they were searching for in the murder of Harry Sage.

▽

11

ON SATURDAY MORNING FRIDAY night was still there. The plywood boards over the broken foyer window, the barricade and wedges holding my own apartment door in place.

Nosy neighbors walked by and stared, not stopping except, finally, Mary Crutchfield, the animal lover. She came up and rang the bell. Rather than move the barricade, I leaned out my bedroom window.

She saw me there and gave me a sharp-eyed look. "Are Snow Ball and Tiger all right?" she demanded in a neighborly but policelike fashion. "Or did they get out in all the ruckus?"

I had no idea where they might be. But the last thing I needed was to be deputized by Animal Mary for a neighborhood posse if the kids' cats were on the loose.

"They're fine," I lied, not knowing. "Couldn't be better."

She nodded approvingly and shuffled down the walk.

"The cats are fine," I heard her announce to old Mrs. Craig who, bless her soul, shot back, "Who cares about the cats? Are the children safe?"

"Yes," I shouted out. "Couldn't be better."

I closed my window and moved the barricade and took the

wedges out and swung the door open to one side. Then I climbed the stairs to Carol's apartment door. Once there, I leaned on her bell until I was sure no one was home. But I was still holding the bell down when I heard a loud scream from Jennifer. Then she was sobbing and crying out for me.

It was horrible.

"Jennifer, what's the matter?" I cried. I took the steps back down in two strides. Jennifer met me, sobbing uncontrollably. In her arms she held the limp furry body of her cat, Tiger. The cat's head fell out of Jennifer's hold and dangled at an impossible angle, the neck broken.

"She was just lying there behind the desk," Jennifer sobbed.

"Oh, no, how awful," I wrapped my arms around her and poor Tiger, trying to encompass both with my protective cover. But it was too late for that. I scooped up Jennifer with the cat and carried her into my bed. When her father and mother died, we had learned how to cry together. And we did that now, crying for poor Tiger. Snow Ball heard us and jumped up and rubbed against us, sensing our feelings as cats do.

Dillon was still asleep and was oblivious to Tiger's death. I consoled Jennifer and we talked about Tiger's life with us. Then I suggested we wrap her body in a clean, soft towel and put her in her sleeping basket until after the Little League game.

As I took Tiger from Jennifer and laid her into the towel, I saw shreds of cloth clinging to her right claw. She had always been a tougher cat than Snow Ball, friendly only to the two children, Carol and me. And if she could get into the office, she slept on my desk. I remembered her swiping at Bruce's silk shirt. I hoped she had gotten a piece of this guy.

I told Jennifer it would be better not to tell Dillon about Tiger until later and she understood.

She was already dressed in her Little League uniform while I was in pajamas and Dillon was still asleep.

"Jay, you're not even dressed yet," she said as she looked

me up and down, making an effort to shut Tiger out of her mind. "The game starts in an hour."

It was true. I knew Jennifer had a game, but I'd overslept and now, if I didn't hustle, we'd be late. And she was supposed to start at first base for the first time in her Little League career.

Carol was also to be at the game. Although she knew nothing about baseball at the time the West Side Little League formed, she volunteered to become one of the three co-coaches for the Zebras. And she took her role seriously. She had been to every game. She said she wanted Jennifer to have the right role model for a coach.

So where the hell was she? I pulled on some Levis and running shoes and a long-sleeved Mets shirt, number 14. Then I finished dressing Dillon—Jennifer had made a good start of it. When he saw my shirt, Dillon insisted on his Mets jacket—it's a ritual costume we have for baseball events, even on television. Finally, we were seated around the breakfast nook, gulping down cereal and orange juice. And Jennifer was able to keep quiet about Tiger's death. I did see her take a peek into Tiger's basket before we left.

I went to the children's room and grabbed the Mets sports bag that had her cap and glove, two baseballs, and a small blanket to sit on. I also grabbed an old black sweater of mine and then made a detour into the office. There I picked Harry's revolver out of the drawer, carefully wrapped it in the sweater, and shoved it into the sports bag under Jennifer's baseball equipment.

Jennifer was waiting impatiently by the door. "Come on, Dad!"

"Let's go," I said cheerily.

It was a beautiful morning. The weather report predicted temperatures in the seventies and the sky was clear and blue. Dillon went running and laughing ahead to the corner. We walked across to the Sailors' Monument and down into the park. Even Jennifer thought it was worth stopping to gawk at the community flower garden. We walked up to 102nd

Street. Two ball fields are squeezed between the West Side Highway and a forty-foot-high sandstone balustrade that divides the middle park from the lower ball fields. Stone staircases at either end lead down to the fields.

Jennifer arrived in time to participate in the Zebras "warm-up exercises"—a practice one of the other coaches, Tom, had instituted over Carol's protest. She'd thought it added to the competitiveness. But she agreed to it when she saw that the need for warming up wasn't necessarily a product of a male-dominated society. These warm-ups had nearly finished when I spotted Carol. She was coming down the stone steps with a Little League player in the Cougar uniform—Jennifer's opponents—and a woman, Judy Sage.

The boy ran out onto the field to get into the warm-ups. Carol, with Judy following her, came up to where I was standing. I didn't know what to say. They appeared exhausted and they were wearing the same clothes they'd worn when they'd left the Balcony Restaurant. What was going on here?

Without speaking, the three of us looked out to where Jennifer and the boy were lining up together, talking and laughing. At a shout from the warm-up coach, they ran, loping along easily.

"Hi, Jennifer," Carol yelled. It was the first thing she said. "This is Harry's mother," she added, pointing to Judy when Jennifer turned to wave hello.

Dillon went racing out onto the field and I ran out to scoop him up playfully and bring him back.

"You been by the apartment?" I asked Carol. Unfortunately, I made it sound like an accusation.

"You know that's none of your business," Carol snapped, as always protecting her independence.

"Well, we got broken into."

That shut her up. She seemed to wilt under the news. Then she told Judy to wait and we walked over to one side so we could talk by ourselves.

"What happened?"

"Somebody was after the records. They did a good job on

our files and split. I wasn't home yet. Meagan locked the kids and herself into my bedroom before he got through the main door. She called the police. But he was gone before the cops arrived."

"What'd they get?"

"I don't know. But there was a casualty. Tiger was killed. He broke her neck."

"Oh, no." Her hand flew to her mouth and she bit on a finger. Tiger and she had never warmed up to one another, but she understood what it meant. "Is Jennifer okay?"

"We had a good cry. I think she's doing fine. You know, it makes you feel violated and insecure. But Tiger got a little piece of somebody. That made me feel a little better."

"Tiger never did like anybody but you and the children."

I nodded toward Judy. "And what's going on here?"

"Judy and I spent the night in a long walk. I've convinced her to leave the Moonies. It was tight this morning when she went back for morning services and breakfast and to pick up little Harry for his game. But she had sold all her candy, and she had to bring Harry junior to the game. I caught something to eat and waited for them on a bench in Riverside.

"After the game they're coming home with me," she went on, "until they find a place to stay."

Jennifer came running up with Harry junior in tow.

"Jay, this is my friend Harry. Jay's my new dad after I lost my real dad," she said to Harry.

Carol had been right. Harry was a darling kid, open and smiling like nothing had happened. He gave me a wave and a "Hi, Jay," and was gone again. His team took the field first.

Tom, the warm-up coach of the Zebras, came up to Carol and shoved a clipboard into her hands. Carol insisted on keeping the tally of players and the innings they played. Everybody had a chance to bat, whether they played or not. Carol also wanted everyone to play equal time no matter how good they were. And each player got a chance to play each position she or he wanted to. It drove Tom crazy and lost a lot of games for the Zebras.

Furthermore, and this helped to even things up a bit, Carol even kept a rudimentary track of which players overplayed on the other teams. For example, the primary coach of the Cougars was a lean bearded guy with glasses named Mark Stein. Mark's son Davey was starting at second base for the Cougars. Davey was a head taller than any other kid on the Cougars and could catch and throw handily for his age. Davey was a ringer. He would have been pitching at a higher level, but this was the peewee division of Little League and a coach on each team did the pitching to make sure the kids could hit the ball. No strikeouts allowed. And Carol knew that Davey had played second base for six innings in each of the last three games.

As Davey made his second putout of the inning for the Cougars, Carol strode purposefully around behind the backstop to where Mark Stein was shouting at his son to "blow them away." I saw her get Stein's attention. Everyone else was watching the game but Stein and Carol were shouting at each other and Carol was pounding on her clipboard, pointing at Davey, who was making the third put-out by catching a blooped ball hit by little Clara Wu. Clara loved baseball but couldn't hit a barn if it were thrown at her.

As the Cougars ran off the field, Carol came back around the backstop to our side—the teams and their supporters did line up on opposite sides of the plate. David Stein looked glum and Carol had a satisfied expression.

"He has to pull the outfielders in," she said with a certain smugness.

"What do you mean?"

"I mean he's played Davey and all the other infielders for the last two games. After the first inning, they're all going to the outfield and the outfield's coming in to the infield."

"Carol, that might cost them the game."

She just smiled back at me. "You know I don't care about winning and losing, Jay."

The Zebras were picking up their gloves to head to the field after Clara Wu's out. Jennifer came right by us.

"Here I go," she said, catching our attention.

"Do your best," I said.

"Have fun," Carol said. "That's what it's all about."

And Jennifer did fine. I'm speaking as an unbiased observer. After the third inning, Jennifer moved to left field to give another kid a chance at first. Judy was watching the game from the Cougars' side of the plate to be with Harry junior when his team was off the field.

Mark Stein was beside himself because the Zebras were in the lead.

Carol came over with a frown on her round face. She gave a toss of her head toward the stone balustrade. "When you have a chance, Jay, look up there on the wall. You'll see a solidly built Korean guy. He's watching the game and he's from the Moonies."

It was easy for me to lift my eyes from watching Jennifer in left field to the high stone wall behind her. Was this whole thing going to spill over into a Little League game?

Carol moved away. And I scanned the wall as casually as I could, as if I were looking up at the people.

I saw the Korean guy. But as my eyes went past him I saw another big guy further down the wall who looked familiar too. I turned back to the game. Davey was at bat for the Cougars and he hit the ball better than any kid there. It was hit toward left, up, up into the air. And Jennifer came in under it and caught it. Everyone gave her a round of applause.

Everyone but me, that is. I was too upset, and looked up at the wall one more time. Yes, the guy I'd surprised in Harry's office was standing there, curly black hair and mustache, taking in the game as pretty as you please.

Carol came back over to stand beside me. "You catch the Korean?"

"Sure, but that's nothing. Look down the wall about ten people until you come to a big man with a black mustache. I last saw him in Harry's office busting a flashlight over my head."

Carol moved away and I went back to watching my kid play baseball. This time very intently. The inning ended and then another. I tried to think while I watched. Was the man with the mustache going to try something in the park? Was the Korean? Every time I looked both of them were waiting, watching. Were they together?

In the middle of the sixth inning I had an idea. I called Carol over. Neither of us had spoken to Judy about the men and she sat on a patch of grass watching Harry junior.

"Here's the thing," I said. "The Korean's watching Judy. The other guy has to be watching me. Can you pick up a rental car? Go by the house and get us some stuff. And one other thing, Tiger's in her sleeping basket. Can you put her in the trunk? Then bring the car down to the West Side Highway. Look, there's an emergency parking area right behind the backstop to the plate. I'll take the kids and Judy out to the Peconic Bay house. We'll get them all out of reach with one fell swoop."

Carol bought the plan. She gave her clipboard to Tom and, with a wide smile, slipped away along the border of the fields past another Little League game. Then she went up the stone stairway at the far end of the games. Neither the Korean nor mustache man followed her.

I tried from then on to look like nothing more than a father who wants to see his kid play a good game.

The innings went too quickly. Although there were lots of people along the upper wall, the two big guys seemed to be the only constant observers. The game reached the ninth inning and the Zebras were coming up for their last shot. They were losing to the Cougars by only eight to seven. I looked up at the wall and saw the mustached man but not the Korean. Then I saw him and he was descending the stone staircase. He was coming right down to the game. He must have kept track of the innings.

Even as I saw him, someone slipped some cold metal car keys into my hand. Carol was there.

"There it is, the red Ford Tempo."

The Ford was parked in the emergency turnoff thirty feet beyond the backstop. In the other direction the Korean was fifty yards away and taking his time, even smiling.

"Time out," I yelled. I snatched up the sports bag with its secret component of one pistol and went right across the diamond to Mark Stein.

"Mark," I told him, "Harry's got to go. Get a substitute."

"What!" Mark exclaimed. The Zebras had gotten their first player to base with nobody out and Harry was now the first baseman. With the Cougars winning by one, Mark wasn't going to let me pull Harry out.

"It's an emergency," I told him. "Harry's got to go now." I glanced up toward the wall. The mustached crook was watching carefully, sensing the unusual. But he was too far away to see or understand. The Korean moved very slowly.

Carol had Judy and Jennifer and Dillon moving toward the Ford. So I said, "Come on, Harry, we've got to go with your mother." He came with me off the field and around the backstop. I looked back and saw the Korean shading his eyes, amazed. And as I looked, he broke into a run.

Mark Stein grabbed my arm. "Hey, you can't take my player!"

"Mark," I said, "if you've ever done anything for me, do it now and slow down that Korean from the Moonies."

Mark looked up and saw the Korean running toward us. He shoved me off and said, "Get going."

I needed no encouragement. I was running and pulling Harry along too, and I didn't look back until I met Carol by the Tempo. When I did I saw Mark throw a great block on the unsuspecting giant, tumbling him down onto the grass. All the parents came up, shouting, blocking the Korean's way as he got to his feet.

I threw the sports bag in front under my feet and told the kids to jump in. They were quick about it, even Dillon. But then Judy balked.

"I can't go," she said, and she started to cry.

"Come on," Carol told her. "Please get in."

"Take Harry, but I have to go back."

With that she bent over into the car and hugged Harry. "Go with Jay and your friends," Judy said. "I'm going to see you in a little bit. Tomorrow or the next day. You stay with them and be good."

Harry wasn't crying but he looked like he might start. "I love you, Mom," he said.

Judy shut the door softly and waved us away. She was trying not to cry and failing.

The Korean had broken through the parents. Carol could deal with this.

"We'll take good care of him," I shouted. I slammed my door and stepped on the gas. The Ford pulled out onto the West Side Highway and in a minute we were going at sixty miles an hour up toward the Cross Bronx Expressway on our way to Long Island.

"That was fun," Jennifer said, and Dillon and Jennifer laughed. But Harry was peering out the back window watching his mother long after she had disappeared.

▽

12

THE WEEKEND HOUSE IS on Peconic Bay above the Hampton Bays. A road turns north several miles before the Shinnecock Canal. It's a straight road for ten miles to a dirt road next to an old red barn on the right. Off the dirt road, a half-mile run, are six isolated houses, the fronts facing the open water of the bay. I rent the fifth one.

We stopped along the way, first to see a *One Hundred and One Dalmatians* revival showing at the Brookhaven Multiplex and then at Pizza Hut. At seven o'clock we arrived, the kids in good spirits after the movie and pizza. As was I, especially from the pleasant memory of the Korean falling over Mark Stein's block.

I carried Jennifer's sports bag inside and tried to call Carol—for the second time, the first had been from the movie theater—but she wasn't home or wasn't answering. I was standing in the kitchen and as I let her phone ring, I took Harry's revolver from the bag and laid it, still wrapped in the sweater, between two boxes of cereal on top of the refrigerator out of sight and reach.

Once we'd settled in, Harry junior became upset again about leaving his mother behind and cried so hard for about twenty minutes that I thought he would never stop. I did the best I could, explaining that his mother had wanted him to come with us. I told him he could count us as his second family if he wanted—just like Jennifer had already done—but he was lucky because he still had a mother who loved him.

It was hard, but he was getting these emotions out. Jennifer saw Harry crying and heard me talking to him, so when he felt better she showed him the Lego blocks and the three of them played happily together until ten o'clock. Then I insisted they go to bed.

Repeated tries to reach Carol were unsuccessful.

After the children were tucked away, I went into the front bedroom facing the water and lay down to collect my thoughts. Instead, I fell into a deep sleep to the open-window sound of water lapping against the beach.

When I awoke, sunlight was streaming into the room. Let the police solve Harry's murder was my first thought when I opened my eyes. If Harry's torturers were going to come after the children and me, they would come up empty. We wouldn't be there.

I rolled over and made up for the sleep I'd missed the last two nights. Jennifer, Dillon, and Harry entertained themselves. Dillon came twice and tugged at my arm but gave up each time I rolled over.

Later, when I was in the bathroom splashing water on my face, Jennifer told me Carol had called once.

"What'd she say?" I wiped the water off with a towel.

"You should have left her a message on the office answering machine."

"That's it?"

"Not to wake you up."

At least nothing was urgent. *That* was something. I picked up the phone and called Carol. No answer. I tried my office. No answer there and the answering machine was off. So much for that idea.

I got the kids something to eat, thanking my lucky stars they hadn't pulled the cereal boxes off the top of the fridge themselves and brought Harry's gun tumbling down. Then I left them to go running down the dirt road to the red barn and a couple of miles south, making a good solid predictable plop, plop, one foot after the other.

When I got back, Jennifer told me Carol had called again.

"Where is she?"

"She said she fixed the window and our door."

"Where is she?" I repeated.

Once more I tried Carol's number without success.

The children and I went outside to play running and laughing games. The rules are that everyone runs after everyone else and then we all fall down and make a big pile laughing. It can be played at any age. Piles of leaves or snow drifts add to the game, but in May we play it on grass. The object is to do this over and over again until you're quite sure that everyone playing loves everyone else playing as much as possible. Harry caught on to the rules right away. He liked it as much as the rest of us.

Harry was just about Jennifer's size—a little over four feet. He had shaggy brown hair and a round face with brown eyes. He smiled a lot. I could see why his parents had fought over custody. Each of them needed him more than he needed them.

Once, in the middle of the game, Dillon left Harry, Jennifer, and me to go into the house to pee. (If only I could get him through every night.)

"Jay, Jay," he screamed when he came out the door. "Carol wants you." He jumped up and down, bursting with the importance of this message, his dimpled smile at its best. I looked at him, puzzled, before I saw that he meant Carol was on the phone.

I ran in to the phone to discover that Dillon had put the receiver back in its cradle, cutting Carol off. I waited, but no call came through. When I called her, there was no answer.

I went back outside with the kids. Later, when we came in at half past three, Carol got hold of me. I tried not to sound annoyed.

"What happened after we left?"

"Judy went back with the Moonies. I tried to convince her not to, and the other parents helped. But we couldn't kidnap her, could we? It's against the law. We may be in a lot of legal trouble already. We don't even know the extent of what we've got. Why add kidnapping to the list?"

"Indeed, why not?" I said, remembering that I hadn't told her about my conversation with Chinless.

"What's that supposed to mean?"

"Remember my task on Friday night—to run down Frederik?"

Carol mumbled her answer.

"Well, I didn't get to Frederik. But I ran into Chinless George. He was part of that Friday-night foursome. He said Harry was dealing drugs."

There was silence at her end. It made me realize that I wasn't mentioning "running into" Harry's other lover, Jackie. I didn't want to mention it. That could be later.

"You mean you murdered Harry because of a disagreement in a drug-dealing partnership?"

I found myself nodding my head at my end. Carol was always quick to put a picture together. "That's what it could look like."

She was quiet and when she spoke she had switched subjects. "I had a carpenter in this morning to rehang your door. Believe me, the next guy won't get through unless he's King Kong."

"You've got nothing new on Harry's murder?"

"Nothing I know of. I talked to Meagan this morning. She gave me the story. You are really, really lucky to have such a great babysitter. What were they after?"

"I think they wanted anything they could get that told them what Harry and I had going. But I'm guessing."

"Did you have the funeral service yet?"

"What?"

"Tiger, the second murder victim of this partnership. You bury her?"

I slapped my forehead. "I forgot you'd put her in the trunk. You think I should with Harry here?"

She thought about that one. "Yes, I think the mutual loss will help him with his own grief. But I'm no therapist.

"And I saw what you meant about Tiger getting a piece of someone. I took a quick look while carrying her to the car. Her claws got enough of the shirt or whatever that she had to have gotten hold of the man in it too. Look for a guy scratched up by a cat."

"Yeah, sounds like the lead that will break this wide open."

"Yeah," she said and she was quiet. "And what about this other lover of Harry's? Jackie?"

"Jackie?" Carol startled me.

"She left a message for you on the office answering machine. I called her back and went to see her. She couldn't tell me a thing."

"You saw Jackie?" I said, amazed. I was also happy Jackie had called. I wished I were in the city so I could see her.

"She said she'd talked to you."

"She did. But I don't think she knows anything we can use. I ran into her while I was nosing around on Friday night."

"Why hadn't you mentioned it?"

She made me angry with the question. "When? While we were avoiding being mugged in the middle of a Little League game? Or when we didn't talk earlier today?"

"She has unusual eyes, Jay. Did you notice?"

"I noticed," I said after a pause. I didn't like Carol noticing too. "Anything else?"

"I'm going up to the Moonies in a last effort to get Judy out of there. Hopefully, she'll be staying with me by tonight. I'll talk to you later. If not tonight, first thing tomorrow."

"I'd rather you called tonight," I said. "I'm isolated out here. We have to keep in touch."

After Carol got off the line, I arranged for Tiger's little funeral.

It was tougher than I thought and maybe it was the wrong thing to do. We got a box and planted Tiger about three feet down next to the blossoming apple tree between the house and the road. Jennifer cried. I cried. Dillon cried. And poor Harry was inconsolable. But, hey, if getting it all out is good for you . . . well, Harry got it all out. And he did want his mom too. I was on the verge of driving back to the city when he settled down and even began laughing and playing games again.

In spite of that, a dinner of grilled hamburgers and homemade chocolate milk shakes was a reserved affair considering there were three kids and only one adult. And after several games of Dillon's Candyland, they all went to bed quietly. I tried to read a book. But I wasn't very successful.

I kept thinking of Harry.

Why had someone wanted to stab him to death? It seemed a torturous death. Not the cleanliness of a professional hit man, but certain. Had the killer thought the job was finished in the first round? Then had there been enough hate and fear to track him down a second time? And enough cold-blooded cruelty to put a knife across the throat? And the finger? Had Harry been tortured?

Harry told me his partner had to be another tax man. Had he meant a tax accountant? Meaning his scam had to do with numbers?

Numbers and big money in an accountant normally added up to embezzlement, not drugs.

But embezzlement didn't seem likely. Harry had been too open and direct. He would have felt me out more if he had wanted to pull me into an embezzlement scheme. Also, the business he embezzled from would have gone to the police. A corporate treasurer wouldn't have stabbed Harry to death because he caught Harry with a hand in the till. Unless Harry was embezzling from the Mafia or something. But the Mafia doesn't go around putting out inefficient contracts. Whoever had killed Harry hadn't been used to killing people.

Harry wasn't embezzling money.

More likely was the corollary to embezzlement. Blackmail.

An accountant handles various kinds of financial transactions. In that process, he uncovers somebody playing financial games with money that doesn't belong to him or her. Then Harry would be in a position to cast stones.

Blackmail payoffs are difficult to trace. Sure, money can come in a brown paper bag. For an accountant, it can turn up as an outrageously high consulting fee from some little company. I saw a case where one company tried to buy out another and the auditors discovered a three-million-dollar overrun in inventory compared to tax statements. The deal fell through, but the accountants ended up with a seventy-five-thousand-a-year do-nothing contract with the firm they had audited. Silence can be golden.

In Harry's case, silence was forever.

But Chinless George had told me Harry dealt drugs. Had Harry intended our partnership to be a laundering operation for the drug money he was pulling in? Tax consulting fees for nickel bags? Drug users deducting their drug purchases as tax accounting bills? A clean explanation of the incoming money making it taxable and "legal" right at the transaction? And a partnership with Jay Jasen, a straight guy who had a friend or two at the IRS itself?

Hey, maybe Harry needed me. I could have been the safety valve. Whoever murdered him seemed to think I was as great a threat. What had Harry said? Had he described me in glowing terms just before he died? You can't kill me because my partner, Jay Jasen, knows all about this too.

"Yes, we can. We can kill you. We can kill Jay Jasen too."

I shivered in my little bed in the Peconic Bay house far from the city lights.

And what about the women? So far there were one wife, two lovers, a secretary, and a prostitute. So Harry liked sex. That didn't make them into murderers. Or did Judy, or Jackie, or Doni murder him in a jealous rage?

Had Carol brought Judy Sage home? Was that just what Judy wanted? Could Carol be wrapping her arms—perhaps literally—around an unstable woman who conspired to murder her husband—or murdered him?

How much did I sleep? Two hours, three hours, I don't know. But Monday morning, Jennifer had the good sense to wake me up when Carol called. It was seven-thirty, bright and early.

"Look, Carol," I said as soon as I was on the line. "Bringing Judy Sage home was a mistake. You can't mix your personal life in a murder."

She was so quiet I thought she'd cut me off.

"Boy, have you jumped to conclusions," she said finally. "It's not what you think. Yeah, she's an attractive woman and she hates men. But there's nothing going on."

"But what if she and the Moonies are behind this or even just the Moonies? Doesn't she give them the leverage to get at us? Jesus, Carol, we're talking about being murdered in our beds. A Trojan horse."

"Sure, I've thought all about it," Carol said. "But it's irrelevant. I couldn't get her. They said she'd talk to me this morning. I'm due there later."

She paused thoughtfully before she went on. "Besides, nobody has actually made an open threat to kill you or me yet. Harry's message was when he was under extreme duress and needed you.

"And," she continued, "having one suspect under our roof makes her easier to watch. Also, if some crazy Moonie is behind it, he'll have to give up if we take away the possibility of getting the money for the life insurance and the business turned over to them. Judy has to cooperate with that. If we can keep Judy out of their clutches, they'll have to give up."

"I don't like it," I said, my paranoia only somewhat abated. "I last see you leaving the Balcony with Judy Sage. Next, by your own admission, you're missing until you show up—with Judy—at the Little League game. Maybe they set her up to keep you away from home while they busted into our office?"

I heard an affirmative grunt at last. I went on with my

attack. "Really, tell me. What happened that took all night?"

Carol's voice took on an indignant tone, nearly angry. "We talked all night. All night! Walking and walking. You ever try to get somebody back from a cult like the Moonies? It's like bringing our partner Harry back from the grave. And it only worked for about four hours until she went back. We're lucky she let us take little Harry.

"Look, Jay, you know I make my emotional and sex life off-limits as topics for us to discuss. But this time I'm making an exception. Just to clear the air, I'm telling you that I've got no interest in Judy Sage. My interest is elsewhere. Okay?"

Carol had something going? "Okay, I believe you," I said. But I felt desperate. I caught myself speaking too loudly and I lowered my voice. "Why don't you give Bruce Scarf a call and see if he's got anything new?"

"He come to work before eight in the morning?"

"I don't know," I said, although I knew he didn't. I found myself annoyed for no good reason I could put my finger on. Perhaps it was my newfound conviction that I could be murdered. Perhaps it was at Carol for forming a relationship with somebody and I didn't even know it was happening. Perhaps I wished I could count on her for more emotional support.

"Do what you can," I told her. And we said good-bye more gently than we had talked.

After that I couldn't stand the waiting. I began to think of friends who knew where the house was. I devised scenarios in which they provided strangers with detailed directions on how to get to me.

Carol called back just before noon.

"There's trouble here, Jay."

I felt my heart sink. "Scarf says they're looking for me," I said, jumping to the worst conclusion.

"No," Carol went on, "Scarf had nothing new for us when I talked to him. It's the Moonies. They got Judy to say she wants little Harry back *tout de suite* or they're going to have her file kidnapping charges against you."

"Shit," I said simply and sincerely.

"Exactly," Carol said.

I started to run off at the mouth. "The police aren't doing anything, that's the whole trouble. Can't we do something active? Can't we get hold of Frederik? Can't we give Scarf the true story so he'll do something? What the hell, Carol. Can't we get off the fucking hook, here?"

"Easy, easy, Jay," she said, trying to calm me down. "Don't forget, Scarf and his boys in blue are going to end their search with you. Do you want that to happen?"

I heard another line ringing in the background. "Hang on, Jay," Carol said. She put me on hold. In a moment she was back on the wire. "It's the Johnsons," she said. "They say you told them they'd have to file by May fifteenth or lose a bundle in penalties and interest. They said you've promised them their return every day and they want some action. Is it ready?"

"No, damn it," I said. "Okay, okay. If I'm coming back I can do it tonight. They can pick it up tomorrow. Tell them they'll both have to sign it and take it to the post office to get a nice clear postmark before midnight. If they could hold off picking it up until the afternoon, that would be great."

"Okay, Jay. I'm calling the Moonies now to let them know Harry will be here. I'll see you when I see you."

She hung up and I went outside to the kids playing on the small beach.

"We have to go home, kids," I said.

"Aw, we don't want to go home," Jennifer said.

"I like it here," little Harry said.

"Don't wanna go," Dillon said.

I didn't remember dead Harry's revolver sitting wrapped in my sweater on top of the refrigerator between the boxes of cereal until we were halfway to New York. And I didn't go back to get it.

▽

13

ARRIVING HOME WITH CHILDREN at midafternoon on a school day was not Julia's idea of a responsible parent. And she took parenting seriously. Dark and angry, she waited just inside the door. I could sense the clicking of her tongue before I heard it. Carol stood in the background. I appealed to her with my eyes but she shrugged to let me know I was on my own, a degenerate father who had kept his daughter out of school for no good reason.

I could see past them into the office. The files which had been scattered on Friday night were now a disorganized stack against the far wall.

When Harry junior came through the door, Julia sat back on her heels slightly. Maybe there was the benefit of a doubt in the woman.

"I haven't told Julia," Carol said directly.

That caused Julia to look from me to her in surprise "Told me? Told me what?" I could see her freeze up. "You two going to do something stupid? You getting married?"

What a relief to have Julia's mind go off in a predictable path. The pressure was off.

"No, Julia, it's that Jennifer and Dillon are in danger."

I could see Julia relax. Protecting children she understood. Carol would always be a mystery.

"You are not telling me anything new," she said. "These children are always in danger around here." But there was a twinkle in those black eyes behind her dark-rimmed glasses. And I could sense her claws retracting.

Jennifer looked up at me. "What do you mean, we're in danger?" she piped up. Harry looked up too, interested even though Carol had had the good sense to leave him out of it.

"He's teasing Julia," Carol told Jennifer. "But you will be in danger if you don't come with me right now." She took Dillon's hand, nodded with her head that Jennifer and Harry were to follow, and led them toward their room.

"I just want to know what he means," I heard Jennifer say as she disappeared.

"Yeah," Harry chimed in, "what does he mean?"

I invited Julia into the office and made her sit in the brown recliner while I sat at my desk.

"Julia," I said, "you saw our new apartment door when you came in?"

She nodded. Her eyes narrowed and I was glad her ninety pounds was going to be on our side.

"That door is new because somebody came through the old one with a chisel and sledgehammer on Friday night."

Julia sat up on the edge of the chair. "Oh, my God," she said as a hand flew to her lips. I had the impression she had always thought something like this would happen.

I told Julia about Harry's murder. I told her that whoever killed Harry also appeared to believe I had something they needed because Harry and I sometimes did business together. They had come here looking for information in my files. My fear, I told her, was they might try to take Dillon or Jennifer to get to me.

Julia's eyes widened at first and then got narrower and narrower until there was just an angry glint of black behind the glasses.

Then I told her about Harry junior and about his mother

being with the Moonies. I told her we were going to have to surrender him to his mother and that's the reason we didn't stay out at the Peconic Bay house.

"Don't worry, Mr. Jasen," she said. "I'm staying right here with the kids until everything is safe. They gotta come through Julia, they wanna get some kids. We just keep all the kids here, right, until this is all over? They don't even go out of the back rooms, right?"

I could have scooped her up in my arms and hugged her. Nothing like a threat to the kids to get Julia's back up.

She stood up out of the recliner. "You should have told me what was happening before," she muttered. She went out, leaving me standing with my mouth open.

Carol came in looking hurt. "She threw me out of the kids' room."

I laughed. "And that's with you on her side."

"I don't think she considers me on her side."

Harry appeared in the office door. "Hey, Carol, is it okay if I get something to drink?"

"Sure. Help yourself, Harry."

"Thank you," he said politely and went running off.

Seeing him made me think of his mother. "You don't think the Moonies got to little Harry do you, Carol? I mean with him having the run of the house?"

I give Carol credit for looking at me with disgust. "Are you kidding?" she said. "Even if you grant the Moonies and Judy herself are all out to get you and me, you can't believe a seven-year-old kid is in on it! And certainly not Harry!"

She was right. I backed off. "Okay, okay. So you're going to save her from Reverend Moon. But tell me again how you can be sure you're not bringing a murderess into our house? She's as likely a killer as anyone else, isn't she?"

"Not for my money, Jay. I spent the night convincing her to leave the Moonies. Even if she is back with them now, I think I'm right about her. She wouldn't hurt a flea."

I stuttered around before I could ask her the next question. Carol drove me crazy with her rule that her personal life was off-limits for discussion. Particularly now . Usually it was a matter of curiosity coupled with some jealous affection. And she knew that. But now it might be critical to life and death.

"Don't get angry with me. I have to ask again, just to be sure. This urge to save Judy doesn't come from an emotional involvement, does it?"

Carol got angry. She swung her head around and narrowed her eyes at me. "For crying out loud, Jay. Are you still trying to determine if I'm sleeping with the woman? First of all, it's none of your business. Now, tell me, are *you* sleeping with her?"

I squirmed. "Come on, Carol."

"Just answer the stupid question."

"No," I said quietly.

"No, what?"

"No, I'm not sleeping with Judy."

"Ah!" she said. "That may give you a feeling for how far off base you are. Well, the answer is no for me too. And I have no desire to." Carol was on her feet moving toward the door. She turned back to me. "What I'm doing for Judy Sage and why I don't feel she murdered her husband are based on an unbiased appraisal not associated with any emotional involvement. You got that?" She walked out and slammed the door behind her.

I felt guilty. Here I was blasting her for an imaginary relationship with this crazy Moonie. Yet I had my own relationship with one of Harry's women to worry about. Jackie. Why didn't I tell Carol about Jackie? Well, I didn't want to. Aside from my elation from our Friday evening together, I had nothing to make me certain it was a relationship. Why hadn't I asked Carol for the number Jackie had left and called her from Peconic Bay? Because I wanted to keep it personal and private, that's why.

And as soon as Carol had left, I played the answering-machine tape for myself and heard the two messages. First came Jackie.

"Hi. It's Jackie. If you need to see me again, here's my number."

She gave the number and that was it. No tip-off that we had anything going except she left her name.

The second message was Valerie Johnson confirming Fred Johnson would pick up their tax return on Tuesday.

I picked up the phone and dialed Jackie's number.

"Jay!" she said when she heard my voice. "Why didn't you call me? No, don't worry. I'm so happy you called now. Why did you go away? I wanted to see you. I wanted to see you very badly."

The words came out in a rush that left me elated.

"I want to see you too." I had reviewed a lot of things to say, but that's what came out direct and honest. No answers to her questions and no small talk of my own.

"Tonight," she said as a statement.

"Okay, meet me at the Silver Bar Café at nine." I figured that would give me time to make dinner for the kids.

I sensed uncertainty in her voice but then she agreed.

I spent the rest of the day floating around the office. Carol came back and worked moodily on her tax projects, but even she couldn't shake my happiness. Or my anticipation.

And neither Judy nor her Moonie friends came to pick up Harry junior in spite of their threat.

The Silver Bar Café was crowded when I got there at nine. Final exams were coming to an end at Columbia and it was a student crowd again. Frederik wasn't there. Neither was Chinless. Monday's not a gambling night and students don't have any money.

Here I was walking into the Silver Bar, Julia was staying the night with the kids, and Jackie, a woman so beautiful that I had trouble looking at her, was waiting for me. I felt like I was deep-sea fishing and hearing the sing of a strike, or looking ahead from a kayak at the rush of white water coming up, or sensing the flow of air when the skis first dip down the slope.

She waited for me at the bar. She wore a red Western shirt with three buttons open, Levis, and black cowboy boots. She smiled openly and looked me in the eyes. My heart was beating and I didn't know what to say. She grabbed me and hugged me. Wanting her, no explanations, I held on tight.

"God, I'm glad you came," she said. She kept one hand around my waist. I had said nothing at all. Her eyes danced into mine, first one and then the other.

I grinned stupidly. "Jimmy," I shouted, "drinks over here." I did it without breaking contact with her eyes. I didn't even look to see if he heard me. But I heard the drinks appearing at my elbow. And I swear we both reached out and took the drinks and walked to a table without ever breaking eye contact.

We touched the glasses and drank.

"Have you . . . " I started but she reached up and touched my lips with her index finger. Then we set our glasses down and held both hands across the table, letting the fingers weave in and out, in and out.

"Let's go," I said. Those were the first words I said to her.

She laughed out loud and her strange eyes sparkled with it. "We walking?"

She only lived four blocks away. "Cab," I said.

"Helicopter if we can get one," she responded, laughing again. I laughed with her, but we were getting to our feet.

We couldn't keep our hands off one another in the short cab ride. "You taste so good," she said after we kissed.

The cabbie got five for a two-dollar fare. And then we were kissing again in the elevator as it rose to the eighth floor.

Her apartment faced Riverside Drive and I sat on the couch trying to control myself. The walls displayed three large landscape oils, two of voluminous clouds and the third of round leafy trees. A Persian carpet was on the floor and the couch was warm leather and goose down. Jackie came back with two brandy snifters and a bottle of Rémy Martin. While I poured, she pulled off her cowboy boots. Then she folded her bare feet under her and sat close beside me. I had undone several more buttons on her red shirt in the cab and as she snuggled up she was very much there for me.

We rotated sips of brandy with long, deep kisses. Her hand under my shirt made little motions that warmed and excited me.

Her bedroom was where she lived. It was larger than the living room. Three walls were covered with bookcases filled with hardcover books. Two more original oil paintings showed nude, middle-aged white people clashing against pastoral Caribbean settings. Track-lighted and inset into the bookcases, they could be seen from the bed.

"Hey, what's all this?" I asked. But she laughed and then was too busy snuggling her lips into my neck to answer and I wasn't interested in her answer right then. She pulled me down onto the bed—a king-size water bed covered by an antique quilt.

Like it is with a new love, I felt like a virgin, excited, out of control. And she was so damn beautiful to look at and she cried in such ecstasy and gripped me with such skill that I climaxed very soon. And we lay huddled in each other's arms, quiet at last in body and soul.

I stroked her hair and looked into her closed eyes. She opened them and looked into mine, smiling.

"Friday was a bad day," she whispered into my ear. "I thought you were a great guy on a bad day. I wanted us to have a good day and see what would happen. This is it."

I blinked. "You don't have someone else?"

She continued looking into my eyes and the little smile left her lips.

"Sure, I've got a lot of someones. I mean men who think I'm the cat's meow. But I don't have *someone.*" She gave me a squeeze and smiled again. "But maybe I've met him."

"And Harry?" I asked. She blinked and pulled back just a few inches away.

"Harry," she repeated. "Harry's dead, Jay. And I'm sorry. But Harry wasn't a nice guy. Yeah, I loved Harry. But

Harry and I weren't going anywhere a long time before Harry died. We just hadn't found a way out."

She stopped and cuddled up close with a contented smile. "And you?"

It was my turn to pause. I was surprised because I thought of Carol Larsing. "No," I said, "I don't have anyone either."

"Then we're lucky," Jackie said. "Here we are, in the same century and close enough in age and both free."

She laughed with delight and I did too. Then we sipped at the brandy. Harry's murder was very distant. So what if someone had broken into my apartment and searched my tax files? No one had tried to come after me. My real worry was to find a trail for the police to follow to the murderer, not to me. The trick was to find out what Harry and I were supposed to have been doing as partners. That was all of it.

"I still don't get it," Jackie said, looking perplexed. "You seem so paranoid that Harry's death means something to you. I don't think anybody intended to kill Harry. Why would they kill Harry?"

I was high enough that if Jackie hadn't used the pronoun "they," I think I would have spilled the beans—my secrets, fears and theories—to her. But, as with Doni, the "they" reminded me of a force out there looking for me.

"Maybe I am paranoid," I said, "but Friday night after I left you I ran into Chinless George. Did Harry ever say anything to you about selling drugs?"

She pulled away again in surprise. "Drugs?" She laughed. "Harry? I'm sure he didn't."

Jackie said it quickly and with so much conviction she had to be right. "Chinless claimed Harry supplied some of the jazz players at the West End and Silver Bar."

"I don't know Chinless," Jackie went on, "but I knew Harry. Believe me, he hated drugs. I think Chinless thought that just because Harry liked jazz. Harry was a jazz junkie, it's true."

I believed her because she was right. I looked into her eyes and she looked into mine. Eye talk. And I lifted her leg and rolled over so I was in her and our eyes were making love and then we were making love with our whole bodies. But the talk about Harry had done something. My rhythm or hers was different. And then for me it was over. I felt what Carol calls the satyr dancing away and leaving me conscious and alone. I was inside a beautiful woman I knew little about except she had been a lover of Harry's.

What the hell was I doing? I wanted to know this woman. I was falling in love with her. But was I screwing it up by being here now? I thought of Harry and I distanced myself from her sexual beauty.

Next I wasn't thinking about sex at all. I was thinking about how upset I was. And then about Harry—the reality of Harry. He must have made love to her like this a thousand times. Her head was thrown back on the pillow and her eyes, open, looked past me in a sexually involved stare—not into my eyes. And suddenly I was hearing the blood gurgling in Harry's throat in her sexual cries and moans.

I took Jackie's arms from around me and pinned them to her sides. Feeling the length of her, her soft breasts and stomach against me and finding her eyes on mine almost kindled a third fire. But not with Harry whispering in my ear.

"Look, it's too soon," I said. She shook her head to free herself from her own ecstasy and looked at me. "I'm sorry. I just made myself upset thinking about Harry. Please let me go and come back for us another time."

She rolled so that I was out of her and beside her. She rested her chin on one hand propped up by an elbow and looked at me. We were quiet that way, then we kissed gently.

"Just go to sleep," she said. "I'll wake you up in awhile. You'll be ready soon."

I shook my head. "I'd love to do that. But I've got two reasons I can't. Two kids, Jennifer and Dillon." It was the easiest lie to give her. Julia staying the night wasn't something she'd know about.

She looked surprised. "Jennifer and Dillon?"

"A babysitter's watching them."

She sat up on the bed. "You didn't tell me you had kids." Then she paused before she said, "And that you're married."

"No, no," I said quickly. "Never married. And the kids aren't mine. I inherited them after my brother and his wife died."

Jackie seemed suddenly distraught. I wondered if I would be able to leave her.

"So that was a babysitter I spoke to on the phone Friday night. I thought it was an answering service. You *really* can't stay?"

I shook my head. Her face was a couple of inches from mine, silver eyes and little teeth.

"It's too soon and I like you too much."

"Then promise me you'll come and stay another time, when things are better? And come again?" She smiled at me and pulled me close to her and rubbed her nipples against my bare chest looking into one eye, then the other.

"Cross my heart and hope to die," I said without thinking.

Jackie gave a little startled gasp and her eyes flared wide. She pulled away. I sat up on the bed and stared at one of the oils: two nude white women on a Caribbean beach, a black teenaged islander bringing them drinks on a tray.

I turned to her. "I'm sorry. I wasn't thinking."

She reached out and gave me a last hug. Then I pulled on my clothes and she followed me to the door. We whispered good-byes to one another as we kissed, and I promised to call her in the morning.

If Harry hadn't died just a few days ago. If Jackie hadn't been his lover. If I hadn't seen his body. Once these things were out of my mind I'd be able to cope with her. And she'd be the greatest lover I'd ever known. I would be back. I wouldn't be able to stop myself.

She opened the door and I slipped out. Her silver eyes watched me through the open crack.

"I think I love you," was the last thing she said.

Then she was locking it and I was stepping into the elevator.

And I thought about Carol again as I floated out onto the street and caught a taxi home. Carol could do whatever she damn well wanted with whomever she wanted as far as I was concerned.

▽

14

TUESDAY MORNING WAS SPENT frantically finishing up the Johnsons' tax return for a noon pickup. While the return was printing on the computer, I rescheduled a couple of audits down at the IRS. There wasn't a minute yet to call Jackie. The Internal Revenue Service doesn't close up shop just because you fall in love or somebody's trying to murder you. No, sir. Carol had gone down to the IRS to cover another client audit. It was just as well. I thought over what I wanted to give her and what I wanted to keep to myself. I didn't feel like giving her anything about Jackie. That meant I had to come up with something new to compensate for Jackie because I felt guilty. I thought it over and decided to come up with the story about the pornography in Harry's bedroom. Maybe she'd see something I had missed.

I was checking the Johnsons' return as Carol came in. Unhappily, I had to call Valerie Johnson and tell her there was yet another error. Could I call her back for a new pickup date? She had no choice but to agree.

I was direct with Carol. She wasn't mad at me anymore. In fact, she seemed relaxed and happy. We chatted about how her audit had gone and then I got straight to the point.

"There was something I left out about my visit to Harry's office the night of the murder."

Carol turned to look at me, cocking her head at an inquisitive angle. I could see she was surprised.

"Harry had a collection of pornography in the nightstand by his bed."

She narrowed her blue eyes but said nothing, waiting for me to continue.

"I didn't think it had anything to do with his murder except now a piece might fit. One of the items was a *Screw* magazine. It was open to the prostitute advertising section and some names were circled with a red pen. One was especially targeted. She had a picture, the face obscured by hair. There was a phone number."

It was too much for Carol and she lashed out at me. "For crying out loud, Jay, are you so threatened by my being judgmental of Harry and, also, of you, that you can't give me all the facts? This could have saved us days."

I tried to defend myself. "You had the black book. You knew they were prostitutes."

"And it was heavy going trying to figure out which ones might be current in Harry's life. Maybe this was the break we needed."

Carol reached deliberately for her desk humidor and took out a Cuban cigar and went through the lighting ritual without saying a word. Then she reached back and turned on the air conditioning exhaust behind her. Next she stood and, leaving the cigar in the ashtray, paced across our rooms, pausing to look out the window into the street behind me.

"What do you think about going back to Harry's office for the *Screw*?" She walked back to her desk, picked up the cigar between her thumb and forefinger, and looked across at me. I wondered what it would be like to kiss a cigar smoker. "Fran Pappas doesn't seem too swift," she went on. "You should be able to manage it."

I found myself nodding at her suggestion. I picked up the phone and dialed Harry's office.

"Hello?"

I recognized the nasal twang and uncertain timbre of Fran Pappas. She wasn't bothering with any office formalities.

"Hello, Fran. This is Jay Jasen. I thought I'd drop by if you're in."

"Oh. Oh! Mr. Jasen. Yes. I've been hoping you'd call. Come over, please. I don't know what I'm doing here. It's so dead. I mean really dead. Oh! I didn't mean that."

"It's okay. No harm done. I'll be able to keep you company for a little while."

I didn't want to give her time to cry again so I got off the line quickly. There would be enough of that when I saw her.

Carol carefully snuffed out her cigar. Then she rummaged through her drawers to find the copies of Harry's partnership.

"Better leave a copy with Fran," she said as she made yet another copy at the Xerox machine. "She may need her own proof that you can hire her as Harry's partner. Otherwise, why should she let you nose around?"

Carol was right, of course. I folded the copy she handed me and stuck it in my shirt pocket. Drugs, embezzlement, blackmail, prostitution—who knew what the devil Harry's partnership would turn up.

"Wish me luck," I said to Carol as I left the office. But Julia stopped me in the hallway. She stood with her arms folded across her chest blocking the way.

"Mr. Jasen," she said. It was always trouble when she called me mister.

I nodded at her.

"Did you forget I have to go visit my doctor today? You remember?"

"Today," I groaned as Dillon came tottering down the hall and threw his arms around my legs. Harry junior and Jennifer were still in school. She was right. She had told me about the medical appointment last week. It might as well have been last year with all that had happened since then.

As Dillon hugged my legs and looked up at me, Julia

turned and went to go out. She paused again after she had opened the door and looked back at me.

"You know, Mr. Jasen, if the kids had a real mother these things wouldn't happen."

She stepped out quickly, so that the door swung shut before I could threaten her with a marriage to Carol. But I didn't have the guts to make that threat anymore. Too much was happening to joke about any of it. Dillon hugged my knees.

"Play horsy with me, Daddy," he said, his eyes big, round, and pleading behind his little glasses. How could I turn him down?

"Carol!" I shouted.

She stuck her head out into the hallway. She had heard it all through the office door and she leaned against the door frame, looking me up and down, at the same time blocking Snow Ball from running into the office with one foot.

"Not me," she said. "I don't want to interfere with a little father-son quality time. I think Fran's the girl—woman—for you. Take him along. Believe me, if I've got her pegged right you'll come back here with a solid marriage proposal. Julia will be quite pleased."

I ignored her as I got Dillon into his Mets jacket. She took the hint and left me alone with him. We got away from her and the lingering odor of cigar smoke.

Fran surprised me. She was pretty, and she had the large breasts *Playboy* had sold and Harry had bought. She was a little on the chunky side from the waist on down, but not enough to hurt the overall picture. Was Fran going to confess that she was another of Harry's lovers?

And Carol's prediction was right on target. Dillon and I hadn't been in Harry's office for five minutes before Fran had her arms wrapped around my neck. The occasion was her renewed breakdown over Harry's death. She was sobbing uncontrollably and I was afraid she was getting the partnership agreement in my shirt pocket wet.

Dillon was attacking some tax returns Fran had left face

up on Harry's desk with an indelible Bic pen—red ink. He liked to say he was doing his tax work and he would scribble ferociously across the face of any paper on my desk. And he was treating Harry's desk no differently. Fran couldn't see him with her head buried in my shoulder.

"Harry was such a great guy," Fran sobbed. "We could have had it all. I could have helped him now that he was splitting up with *that* woman."

I confess I wondered if she had any idea of the possibilities. "Judy?" I asked her tentatively.

Fran nodded, crumpling the partnership agreement slightly with her chin. Unrequited love had become unrequited grief. She dissolved into more tears. And I didn't mind holding her close. But at the increase in volume, Dillon looked up from his "work."

"What's the matter?" he asked. "Why's she crying?"

It was enough to warm poor Fran's heart to the point where she could tear herself away from me for him.

"Oh, he's so cute," she said. "I'd like to have a little boy like you."

She crouched down and tried to gather Dillon into her, something he wasn't about to let happen without a good fight. He pushed away from her to get back to the desk.

"I hope you'll feel that way when you see what he's been doing to those tax returns," I said. I did not mention that Dillon needed a mother.

And Carol had been right on her second prediction. Dillon provided a perfect cover for my real work. While Fran was attempting to jolly him into accepting her, I excused myself and made for Harry's bedroom.

But I was too late. The porno books and the copy of *Screw* were gone from the nightstand. There was a framed photograph of Harry with Harry junior. I slipped it out of the frame and took it with me.

And Carol was going to be proud of me. Since I couldn't get what I'd come for, I set about seeing what we might salvage from Harry's business if we ended up buying it. I made a list of business tasks for Fran so that we could evaluate and transfer Harry's accounts. Only after I'd projected this professional approach did I get back to the subject of Harry himself.

"By the way," I said, and I hesitated, not wanting to get off on the wrong track with Fran.

"What is it, Mr. Jasen?" she asked.

"Please call me Jay," I said with a magnanimous wave of my hand. "Harry had a weakness," I went on. "I wouldn't want anyone to know about it. He liked to buy, you know, some of that sex junk. You know what I mean, pornography? Funny about Harry. He wasn't really like that—"

"I know, I know," Fran cried and it set her sobbing again. I had wisely sat down and put the desk between us. She grabbed up Dillon instead, but he broke away and ran around to jump up into my lap, now staring at Fran suspiciously.

"You would have helped Harry by taking care of anything like that so no one would know, right?"

Fran stopped crying and looked shocked. She could really turn it off and on.

"Of course," she said. "I got rid of all that stuff."

"What did you do with it?"

"Oh. Well, I had it in a garbage bag here. When I heard the garbage truck outside this morning I went out and threw it all right into the truck." She smiled. "The sanitation men kidded me about doing union work. It went right into the thing that rolls up into the truck."

"Good job," I told her. What else could I do?

Nothing unusual emerged from looking through Harry's files. But then, I hadn't expected anything from the legitimate side of the business. Someone had already taken care of that too. Maybe I was severely underestimating Fran. On the phone I had taken her to be fat and insecure. She wasn't fat. Maybe she wasn't even insecure. Maybe she spent her spare time murdering men she worked for.

I took the wrinkled partnership agreement out of my

pocket and tried to unfold and straighten it as best I could. I gave it to Fran and told her to show it to anyone who asked why she was working here for me. Then Dillon and I were able to get away with nothing more than one additional crying jag divided about equally between us. I assured Fran that she was on our payroll now and not to worry. She saw us out the door, closing it only after we were well down the sidewalk.

When I got back to the office, Carol wasn't there. But Julia had already returned from her doctor's appointment. I was able to turn Dillon's care and feeding over to her.

At last I had a little time alone. I called Jackie.

"How about tonight?"

She laughed and I loved the sound of it. "You can't get enough of me," she teased.

"That's right, that's why I have to see you tonight. I've thought of nothing all day but seeing you."

Jackie laughed a second time. "You poor man, I can't see you tonight."

Immediately I conjured up an image of another man in her life. "No?"

"Don't worry. There's not another man," she said as if reading my mind, "but I have to meet a girlfriend who's having some troubles. How about tomorrow night? Making you wait a day will make our second time together more delicious."

I thought of her eyes looking into mine, first into one eye and then into the other, silver eyes.

"I love you," she told me at the end. "And don't worry, we'll see each other tomorrow."

I hung up standing on a cloud from which I had trouble reaching down to do my tax work. Carol came back just at that moment.

"What happened?" she asked. I thought she was referring to Jackie and I was astounded she had found out about us. But then she went on, "Fran give you the goods?"

"Oh. Oh!" I said, almost a mimic of Fran. "Nothing."

"Nothing?"

"Fran had thrown the stuff away. Thought she was protecting Harry."

"It figures. Nothing's working for us."

"Let's give *Screw* a call. We can order up the back issues."

Carol looked at me. "Good idea, Jay." She picked up her phone and took care of it. She asked them to send up a dozen random issues for the past two years. *Screw* refused to send a messenger but a COD UPS package would arrive within the next couple of days.

I was very pleased with myself, being in love *and* having a creative idea all at the same time. I think I must have had a smirk on my face because I caught Carol looking sharply at me.

That evening I decided to do a little research on my own. I took a cab out to the exotic dancer lounge called Gold Girls in Queens. They advertised three floors of the world's most beautiful women. I had Harry's picture with me when I paid my cover and took a seat at the main bar. There wasn't much in the way of light except on the three women wearing almost nothing dancing on a circular stage. I did a double take. Charlene was dancing there wearing nothing but a G-string of white linen with a Western fringe. My God, she was good-looking and had a great smile too.

The set came to an end and the women put the rest of their costumes back on, coming down off the stage while others went up. Charlene had a matching linen bra with a Western fringe and a pair of ripped Levi short-shorts. She also pulled on some black cowboy boots that I had seen her wearing at our place.

I was torn between rushing out so she wouldn't see me and talking to her. But she spotted me as she came down off the stage.

"Hi, Jay," she said brightly. She seemed as surprised as I was. "What are you doing here?"

I stuttered, not knowing what to say. But she came in first.

"Look, do me a favor. Don't tell Aunt Carol you saw me here, okay. I don't want her getting upset."

"I don't know. I'll have to say something. I'm too close to her not to. I know she'll have a problem with this. But she believes in independence. Give her, and yourself, a chance."

She rolled her eyes. "Okay, Jay, just give me a week to tell her myself."

"It's a deal if you can help me out." I took out Harry's photo. "You know anyone who's worked here for six months or more? And did they ever see this guy around?"

Charlene looked at the picture. "Let me ask Mel," she said. "She's been around."

She called over another woman who'd finished a tabletop dance. She had her bra off and I was looking closely at breasts so firm and well developed she had to be injecting silicone. I concentrated on my photograph.

"What's up, Freddie, " she said to Charlene.

"Freddie's my stage name," Charlene explained to me. Then she turned back to Mel. "This guy's a friend of my aunt. He's trying to find somebody who knows the guy in this picture."

I held out the picture, trying to look only into Mel's face.

"Harry Sage," she said. "I went home with him a couple of times."

Jackpot at first try. "You get to know him well?"

Mel laughed. "Anybody here wanted to get to know Harry got to know Harry. You know what I mean?"

I tried to laugh with her but it stuck in my throat. Some guys were calling for Freddie and another table was shouting for Mel. They went back to work.

As for me, that was all I could take for the night. But on the way out I had to pass Charlene dancing almost nude on this table for six men. She arched her young Bardot eyebrows at me.

"Remember," she shouted. "A week!"

I nodded and gave her a wave.

▽

15

WEDNESDAY MORNING I WAS up early to finish the poor Johnsons' tax return. Hey, nobody's perfect. So I missed the promised date with one tax return. I didn't count on the fact that I'd find an error when I did the final check and have to correct several entries. Fred Johnson said he'd try to slip it through on his Pitney Bowes machine with the prior day's date. I don't approve of that kind of thing, but it's his business. I'd told him we'd cover the increase in penalty. And I did finish the corrected return except for the reprinting and had about fifteen minutes before the kids were due to wake up. I had time to get to the newsstand for a *Times* to relax over while Dillon, Jennifer, and Harry worked on their breakfasts.

Harry junior was still our guest after three days. The longer the better as far as I was concerned. Jennifer and I had both gotten good at helping him through his bad moments and, all in all, he was as healthy as any of us.

Outside, it was a dream day. The sky was a sharp blue broken by pure white cumulus clouds and a fresh breeze came up off the Hudson that reminded me I lived in a great ocean port with all the romance of distant places. I had a spring to my step, and I had to slow down not to bounce right over the top of Mr. Patel's newsstand. Patel gave me a funny smile when I asked for my ration of a *Times* and a *Newsday* as if he were acknowledging one of us was in love and we both knew it wasn't him.

Not only do I never whistle but also I can't stand people who do. I confess, though, I was whistling as I walked back to the brownstone from Broadway. Julia passed me on her way to get some milk and orange juice and I guess my mood was so infectious that she smiled at me herself.

As I pushed open the foyer door, my newspapers under my arm, I heard someone coming down from Carol's apartment.

I'd like to say that I discreetly look the other way when one of Carol's lovers comes down the stairs in the morning. But, human nature being what it is, I don't. I want to know who she's sleeping with. Honoring one another's private lives is important. But not talking to Carol about relationships and not keeping my eyes and ears open are two different things.

As I turned to open my door I glanced up and saw that Carol had her back to me and her arms wrapped around someone she was kissing a fervent good-bye to. I hesitated just a second, unseen. The two of them swayed slightly and I could tell Carol's lover was a woman.

The woman broke the kiss and peered down at me. I could see her face. The woman was Jackie. And she saw me too.

Carol slipped away from her and back into the apartment, closing the door without knowing I'd seen them.

I had left my apartment door open a crack and now I stepped in and pulled it firmly closed behind me. I stood just inside, listening. I could hear her take a step and pause. She came back to the door. I stopped breathing. She moved away again and I heard the street door open and close. She had gone. I rushed into the office to the front window and saw her walking straight by, her head up but her eyes looking wild and disturbed. I threw myself into the recliner and pushed back so hard that it almost went all the way over. I cursed violently. I leapt to my feet and started dumping books and tax returns onto the floor. My jealous rage came to a halt with the demise of an old but much-loved vase lamp. The shattering sound brought me up short.

"You okay, Dad?"

I looked up from bending over the shards and saw Jennifer standing in the door.

Children have their own way of loving you and making you feel okay even when you're not. I went to her and knelt down and folded her into a big hug. I found it impossible to describe to a seven-year-old the feelings of a jealous rage. Or the rationale.

"I'm okay, Jennifer," I said, "because I love you."

"I love you too, Dad. Don't be sad."

She stroked my hair with the soft touch of a child. I felt a lot better.

"Come on," I told her, "breakfast time. Let's wake Harry and Dillon if they're still asleep."

Fifteen minutes later the four of us were gathered around the kitchen breakfast nook going through our usual morning chatter. But I was not reading either newspaper. The confrontation with Jackie was pushing down on me like a heavy weight. And I had to face Carol.

Julia arrived back from the store. Shortly she was shepherding Jennifer and Harry off to school and Dillon off to a play date with another three-year-old.

I was left to sit alone and stare at the wall, waiting for Carol. I did busy myself with a little cleaning up—tasks I didn't have to think about—the broken lamp, the books, the tax returns that I'd scattered. But that didn't take long enough. I started a number of letters to Jackie ranging from the damn-you category to I-can't-live-without-you. Each one ended up scrunched into a little ball in the circular file. Then I switched to a letter to Carol but that followed the others.

The hell with both of them.

Carol arrived late. She breezed into the office floating on air, it seemed.

"Jay," she said, "I think I've fallen in love."

I was out of there. I got to my feet without a word to her and crossed to the door, managing myself very well, I thought. I picked up a light jacket and closed the office door quietly behind me. I heard her calling my name as I closed the front door and walked off down the street.

I walked over to Riverside and down inside the park and I had passed the boats at the 79th Street boat basin before I had a thought in my head.

Then it came to me, simple as it was. I had to get away from Carol. One way or another she had been messing up my life ever since she walked into it. Now she was stealing my lover.

It was dark when I got back to the brownstone. I knew Julia had planned to stay the night, so I wasn't being totally irresponsible. But I must have followed the trails Judy and Carol had left across the city on Friday night. I became more and more determined. I had to get Carol out of my life.

Carol was no longer in the office but the odor of cigar smoke lingered there. Thank God, I thought, I won't have to put up with cigars.

I could hear Julia and the children in the back, but I didn't go to see them. Not just yet. Rather I went back out into the foyer and looked up the stairs toward Carol's door. It was a long climb but I made it. Then I found myself ringing her doorbell. She answered quickly enough. And she was very alarmed.

"Jay," she said, "what's wrong? Why did you just leave like that?"

"Can I come in? We need to talk."

Carol moved back, holding the door open. She followed me as I led the way into her living room. Her three white couches were there, still forming the sides of the square, the fourth being the wood-burning fireplace she'd had restored when the brownstone had been redone. It hurt to think that she and Jackie had probably made love right on these couches. But the thought caused me to be direct with her. I sat down on the couch facing the fireplace, then moved to another when she sat on the same one. I had rarely been in Carol's apartment.

"Carol, I can't take it anymore. We have to break up our business and our friendship."

Her eyes widened and she wrinkled her nose and swung her blond hair around her head. It was the first time something I'd said about us shocked her. She leaned forward on the couch very deliberately.

"Jay," she said softly, "I didn't know you felt that strongly about me."

She had misunderstood. I shook my head at her. Something I was always doing in everyday disagreements.

"It's worse than that," I told her. "This morning I ran into the woman who spent the night here last night—"

"Jackie!" Carol broke in. "And you think I'm using poor judgment by getting involved with someone who knew Harry." She was beginning to turn her uncertainty into anger now. "Well, it's not like that, Jay—"

"I love her!" I shouted at Carol, for being so stupid and for thinking I was so damn predictable. It certainly cut her short in midsentence.

"I love her." She repeated my words like an English lesson. She sat stock still, trying to comprehend what I was saying. "You mean we're in love with the same woman?"

I nodded.

"You, ah, slept with her?" she went on in the same quiet voice.

Again I nodded.

To her credit, in an instant Carol was able to jump to the same conclusion it had taken me all day to work out.

"Well," she said, and she sat back in the couch staring straight ahead. I was quiet while she worked it out in her head. "We can't be rivals and work together," she said.

I stood up.

"Can't we talk?" she said. She did have tears in her eyes.

I couldn't speak until I coughed once. "No," I said then. "I've thought this through and it's what has to happen. I'm sorry." I only paused a second and then went on so she wouldn't have time to argue. "I'll start dividing up the files in the morning. Once we've sorted out whose clients are whose we can go from there. I don't think there's much point in talking until I've done that."

Carol looked up at me. She seemed hurt. "I'll come down and get some work to bring up here," she said, "unless you want me to help you."

"I think the less I see of you, the better right now," I told her. "Maybe next week we could work out more of the details."

She shook her head slowly in confusion. "You seem bewitched by her. I'm not like that—but I, too, must see where that relationship between her and me is going."

Carol didn't show me out, she just watched me go, sitting there by herself facing her fireplace, still not quite grasping what had happened.

I would have thought all that business about Jackie and Carol and Jackie and me would have been enough for one day. But it wasn't.

I was sitting in my office after dinner and the children had been tucked in for the night. I'd sent Julia home because, in spite of her promise, there was no reason for her to sleep over. Besides, I wanted to be alone. It was only about ten o'clock and I sat there in the dark room thinking about Jackie and Carol and pretending it was the last thing I wanted to think about. Then the phone rang. Ordinarily the answering machine would have been on to screen the call. And if it wasn't, I wouldn't have answered it. But I felt like talking to someone, anyone, even if it was a client with a stupid question about an Individual Retirement Account. I hoped in my heart that it was Jackie. I answered it.

"This is Melissa. You remember me, don't you, honey?"

"Sure," I said. I'd forgotten for a few hours that the police were after me and someone was trying to kill me and I wasn't sure I wanted to be reminded.

"There's some stuff coming down over here. You know what I'm saying?"

"Maybe. What's happening?"

"Oh, no," she said, "I need some help with this one, big boy. You gotta come over here. Okay? You gotta dig me outta this one."

"I'm tired of Harry and all his crap," I heard myself saying. "You gotta dig yourself out. I've had it." I slammed down the phone.

I could feel my spirit sinking. Harry and all his stuff was too much for me now. What was I doing turning down an offer that might tell me something to clear me? I dug out the black book and called Melissa back. The line was busy.

I'd go over there—it was what she had asked me to do. But I had a problem. Julia had gone home. I could hardly go running up to Carol's to ask her to suspend our separation so she could babysit while I tracked down a prostitute lead. Who knows, maybe even Jackie had slipped into Carol's and that was the last thing I could handle. If I went up there and ran into *her* . . .

It took me forty minutes to locate Meagan and get her over. As I left I told her not to answer the phone or the door.

When I got to Melissa's building on East 50th Street the winking doorman let me go right up after he heard the magic apartment number. I stepped out of the elevator and started down the hall. At the same time I saw Cheryl coming toward me from the apartment. She was wearing a mink coat and looked upset. She didn't look at me as she passed and I had to turn to catch her by the arm.

"Cheryl?"

She looked up and back at me, furtively. I don't think she had any memory of me.

"I'm Jay Jasen," I said. "I was here to see Melissa last Friday. About the guy who was murdered. She in there? She said she had something for me."

Cheryl shook her head and continued moving down the hall away from me. Suddenly she stopped and came back and grabbed my arm.

"Quickly," was all she said and I was moving alongside of her, being led actually, into the elevator. It was still there from my coming up. We stepped in and the doors closed and we were alone.

"Melissa's dead."

"Dead," I echoed in disbelief.

"I was upstairs with a john and when I came back she was in there dead. She's in the bathtub with her wrists slashed. It looks like suicide, but I don't believe it. Somebody killed her."

"I want to take a look," I said.

She shook her head. "Somebody called the cops," she said. "The phone was off the hook and a 911 operator was on the line. That's why I'm getting out and not coming back."

As we stepped into the building lobby, a police car pulled up and an ambulance joined it. We turned west on the sidewalk. The doorman was busy greeting them and I'm sure he never saw us leave. We got as far as the corner of Third Avenue together when Cheryl stepped out and flagged a cab.

"You have somewhere I can reach you?" I asked her.

She looked back at me as if I was crazy. "No," she mouthed and she closed her eyes as if to shut out everything she'd ever done on 50th Street. Then she was gone in that cab and I knew she was one woman I'd never see again.

I looked back and saw another cop car pulling up to the curb. I hustled along the sidewalk, turning up Third Avenue to get Melissa's death out of sight and out of my mind. But I couldn't stop thinking about her.

So what was the deal here? Had I been set up? Had Melissa been conned into calling me and then murdered so that I'd be caught at the scene? But she didn't know I was going to show up. No, she must have called someone else after she called me. And the other person she called had killed her. Except for Cheryl, no one had seen me. No one but the doorman. At least it wasn't me who was dead! Perhaps I was still safe from murder myself because the case for my taking this rap was being carefully built.

▽

16

THAT NIGHT WAS THE worst of my life. Melissa kept trying to bend over me and whisper in my ear, "You know what I'm saying?"

Jackie lost. Carol gone. Harry dead. How could I handle it all? Go to the police? Sit up with a gun? I didn't have a gun and Harry's was on top of the refrigerator at the Peconic Bay house. Maybe I should run back out there again? Maybe I should get a calculator close at hand. That's what I carried, not a gun. Throw some tax numbers at the killer.

I knew one thing—I wasn't thinking clearly.

The next morning I went through the rote exercise of getting Jennifer and Harry ready for school and Dillon dressed. After Julia had taken them, I went into the office and examined the task of getting rid of Carol and her business for something to do—the least bad of the terrible alternatives.

We had a big business. I spent the morning making stacks of Carol's files for her to move out. Since I wasn't giving up the apartment even with Carol as landlord, the business address would remain the same for both of us. That alone would cause less disruption. But it was going to be hard to explain our separation to old friends and clients.

The phone only rang twice. First, Fred Johnson wanted to know where the hell his tax returns were. I assured him again that I would cover any penalties I caused. He grumbled a lot but there was nothing he could do.

The second call came from Doni. Could I meet her for lunch?

Sure Melissa had been murdered. But her death affirmed in my mind that "they" weren't out to kill me. And meeting with Doni had an advantage of its own. She was beautiful too. She would take my mind off Jackie. Hey, what was happening? Was I becoming Harry, taking over his women one by one?

But I was able to concentrate after her call although I found myself counting the minutes until one o'clock.

It was raining as I flagged down a cab, a summer drizzle you wouldn't notice until it soaked you through.

At Johnny's Place, Doni wasn't outside. No one was. Rain doesn't lend itself to sidewalk dining. I had no intention of giving up feeling sorry for myself, but I'd forgotten Doni's beauty.

She had on the bracelets, mostly silver but some gold. She must never take them off. She had abandoned the wire-frame glasses and the frizzy brown hair was kept in control by a black fedora. A light fuchsia mascara did amazing things to her eyes. She wore a marcasite pendant earring in the one ear and a circular silver and black onyx in the other.

Her jacket was from a man's black tuxedo. She had studded the lapels with rhinestone patterns. Beneath it she had on a man's white ribbed undershirt. She'd matched the coat with a tight black skirt. She had changed perfumes and this one went well with the fuchsia mascara—maybe a scent called Spring Fuchsia?

I was feeling a great deal less sorry for myself as I slid into the seat facing her.

"What have you got?" I asked. I wasn't going to beat around the bush even if she was good-looking.

"I don't know. Maybe you could use some help." She

picked up a business card she had out beside her plate and handed it to me. I looked it over. It said Judith Steinberg, Attorney at Law.

"How can she help?" I said too quickly and harshly. Then I softened up a bit. "She a friend of yours?" I wasn't much interested.

"No," Doni said, "it's me."

I sat back, looking at the card closely. Maybe all the names in Harry's black book weren't whores.

"Doni is sort of a nickname," she went on. "It's, well, a nom de plume."

I suppose I got brutal again, but I wasn't in my best mood. "You mean a nom de guerre, don't you?"

She cocked her head at me, either as a question or in alarm, I couldn't tell which.

"Why?"

"We found a black book on Harry."

She stared back at me as if unknowing. "A black book?"

"Of names. All women's names. Yours was among them."

"I don't understand."

"It appears the others were all prostitutes."

Her face flushed and continued to redden as she recognized exactly what I was saying about her. She reached over and plucked her card from my fingers. She did it as she rose and then she was heading for the door.

I was a victim of the surprise I'd created and I watched her until the door had closed behind her. Then some feeling of self-preservation made me leap to my feet and run after her.

Doni stood by the curb in the rain, one arm raised for a taxi. But even a beautiful woman can't get a cab in New York City in the rain. The tears were streaking down her face, ruining her mascara and making her appear very, very vulnerable. I wanted to touch her, to comfort her.

"I'm sorry," I said. She twisted toward me as if my voice had touched her physically and she was full of revulsion.

"Sorry!" she screamed. It was hard for her to be derisive

while crying her eyes out. She turned and stalked away, walking along outside the parked cars in the street. I followed behind her.

I was also shouting. "What was Harry's game? I'm losing my business, my friends, my lovers—my life. All over Harry's game. I don't know what the hell he was doing. Do you?"

She turned back toward me. The rain had suddenly picked up and except that the fedora protected her, I couldn't be sure whether it was tears or rain on her face.

"You think you're the only one losing a life, Jay Jasen? I stumbled into doing it for the money and stumbled out again. Can't I get away from it? Yes, my nom de guerre was Doni. But it isn't anymore. She's dead, you son of a bitch. And if I'm not careful, you'll have her kill Judith Steinberg too."

She was screaming. I knew the high pitch in my voice showed clear frustration and fear. With effort I lowered my voice.

"Did you know a woman called Melissa?"

Something made her stop and turn again. Was it just the change in my tone?

"Light-skinned black woman?" I went on.

"No, so what? I'm out of it. My straight life won't survive this stuff coming back." Her voice had lowered also.

"She's dead. I met with her about Harry and now she's dead. They made it look like suicide, but I'm not fooled."

"Maybe it was? Maybe you're building all this up in your mind."

"She had called me earlier to tell me she had something for me. I think she tried to make a deal and lost."

Doni was looking me in the face, searching into my eyes. Suddenly she reached out and took my hand. It was a complete flip-flop.

"You're scared," she said.

I felt the air go out of me like a popped balloon. "Yes, I'm scared. Harry's dead. Melissa's dead. I've been close. How do you know you're not on the list?"

She shook her head. "I don't think so. I'm out of it. Why would I be?"

I said nothing, just did my own searching of her eyes as Jackie had taught me to do, one eye and then the other, asking. She was holding my hand and she squeezed it.

"I live five blocks from here. Come with me."

Ignoring the rain didn't mean we didn't get wet. We were two bedraggled-looking birds by the time we got to her place. She excused herself and came back in a sheer white silk robe that left nothing to my imagination. She came up and put her arms around me and kissed me. I responded for a moment and then I pushed her back. She could turn me into an emotional whirling dervish if I let her. Too much had happened.

"I'm sorry and I'm flattered," I said. "You're very beautiful and at any other moment in my life we'd be rolling on the bed in two minutes. But not today."

She conceded with a look of her eyes. Then she disappeared again and when she came back she had another silk robe—a man's in red with black lapels. She sent me into the bathroom to get out of my wet duds. I hung my clothes over the shower curtain and emerged dressed in the robe.

She took my hand as I came out and led me to the couch where we sat beside each other. She wore only her earrings, bracelets, and the white silk robe. I wore only the red-and-black silk robe. I did wish it was another time—the place would do just fine. She sat holding my hand looking into my eyes.

"Tell me about the black book," she said, nodding encouragement. "If you can think of me as Judith Steinberg and leave Doni behind, maybe I can really help you."

"It's an address book with the names of two to three hundred women. The ones we've reached by phone will try to make a date for sexual adventure for pay. Other numbers are disconnected or wrong. I've only talked in person to two of them. You and Melissa. She's dead."

Doni thought about that. "Why don't you give me the

book?" She saw me flinch. "I mean, you could Xerox the pages for me. What have you got to lose? I know women who do this and you don't. I may have worked with them. Maybe I would recognize someone who would have a reason to kill Harry."

As she said it, Doni's eyes took on a deadness, like glass. It seemed to me that anyone who had worked much as a prostitute might become brutal in spite of how much she thought she had left it behind. An involuntary shiver went up my spine as I looked at her.

She turned and smiled at me, her eyes coming alive again. "Don't you think it might be some help?"

I agreed. She was to come to my office the next day to pick up a copy of the book. But after that look I saw in her eyes, I just wanted to get out of there. I lied and said I had an appointment to get back to. I went into the bathroom and changed back into my clammy clothes with the door closed. Then I left, and we didn't kiss good-bye.

▽

17

I WAS IN FOR a surprise when I got back to the office. Judy Sage was sitting in the brown recliner and the large Korean—the Little League fan—was going through my files. I assumed he represented Moon's organization.

"Hello," Judy said too brightly. "I hope you don't mind. Julia let us in but said we'd have to wait for you before she'd let us take Harry junior. He's playing with Dillon in the back. We told her we'd wait here."

I gestured toward the big guy going through the files. "Is that your idea of waiting?"

He stopped his work to look up and take me in. Even though he could see that I didn't match his size, he still seemed to puff himself up with the full power of his church.

"Mrs. Sage has the right to look through her husband's records. You have tried to pull the wool over our eyes."

He had a thick Korean accent that made him sound funny. But he didn't look funny. And if he was Moon's hit man to free up a new convert's inheritance through the murder of her husband and possibly her husband's business partner, I had better take him seriously.

"I don't know who is pulling the wool over whose eyes," I said to him. But I wasn't going to take on this guy alone.

Carol, I thought, could make short work of him. I turned to Judy. "Is Carol upstairs?"

"I don't know," she said.

"Could you see? Ask her to come down if she is?"

She glanced at the Korean, but he evidenced no obvious displeasure and Judy went for Carol.

While she was gone, he folded his arms across his chest and began to rock back and forth on his heels. An eerie sound filled the room and it was a moment before I placed it. The Moonie was humming.

Carol came down with Judy trailing behind. She frowned when she saw the Korean.

"What's going on here?"

"That is the question we wish to ask you," the Korean said, stabbing a finger violently at Carol. "You tried to kidnap Mrs. Sage. You've held her son against her will. And now you won't show us our files."

I was furious. "Show you *your* files! You never asked. You broke in here and ransacked our office. . . . "

But the Korean was already waving an official-looking document. Even from where I stood I recognized it because I'd seen Carol waving it just a week earlier and standing where he was standing. It was the partnership agreement between one Harry Sage and myself—that is, the copy I'd signed, Carol had notarized, and then left with Judy and the Moonies.

"Mrs. Sage could hardly break into her own husband's office. This paper says Mr. Jasen is Mr. Sage's business partner. We are looking in our own office."

The oriental accent reversing *l* and *r* almost turned the crisis into a comedy in spite of the ethnic stereotype implied, but it wasn't hard to keep from laughing. Carol was as helpless as I was in the face of this guy's attack.

Next he gestured toward the rear of the house. We all understood that he meant the gesture for Judy.

"Get little Harry. There is no reason to stay in this terrible place any longer. Our Father needs us."

Judy disappeared obediently.

"You won't get away with this," Carol said. But the Moonie closed his eyes and rocked back and forth and the eerie sound filled the room once more. I could see Carol's eyes widen as the humming came through to her.

Judy reappeared with Harry in tow and the big Korean had her ask for the keys to Harry's office. Carol handed them over without a single word of complaint. Then the big guy led his little band to the door.

"Aw, Mom, why can't we just stay here?" Harry said. "They said they'd let you stay too."

Judy looked wildly back over her shoulder at us.

Harry looked back at us too, and shrugged his shoulders. "Good-bye, everybody," he said waving. He was the only polite one in that bunch.

"Come back and see Jennifer soon," I shouted. He gave me a last smile and waved again as he disappeared out the door.

Carol seemed as stunned as I was at the swiftness of the Moonie attack and its success. He not only had retaken little Harry as a prisoner, but he also thought he had established his right to return at any time with Judy's permission to go through our files as the successor to Harry's business interests.

Carol sighed and turned to look at me. "Do you have any good news, Jay?"

"Like?"

"Like none of this is happening to us?"

I shook my head slowly. She left me without another word.

Now alone, I saw the package in a plain brown wrapper on my desk. Inside, there were twelve issues of *Screw* magazine covering random dates over two years. I laid them out on the floor. Just at that point, of course, Julia came barging in to tell me she was on her way to pick up Jennifer. She was outraged when she saw the sex magazines spread out. She stormed out of the house taking Dillon with her.

Going right back to my task, I quickly found the "Jacqueline" ad that I'd seen on Harry's bed stand. Long hair obscured her eyes, but even with the change in hairstyle, I could identify her from the teeth. Harry's lover, Carol's lover. My lover. Harry had known. Was that how he first found her? I dialed the number given in the ad. A machine answered the phone and it was her, Jackie.

"Hello there. This is Jacqueline. I really want to get your call. So you can leave a message with your first name and the exact time I should call you. I will call you back. And don't worry, I'm so discreet that only you will know it's me. I'll ask for Mr. Smith. If it's you, you'll know. If it's somebody else, it's a wrong number."

I checked and the phone number I had for Jackie was not the same.

I couldn't deny that I still wanted her. Maybe there was some explanation she could give me. That is, if we ever talked again.

She had advertised in three of the older issues. But she had stopped advertising for the last year. Still, the phone number worked.

I took Harry's black book and compared it to the numbers listed in the advertisements. Many of the advertised names matched up with numbers in the book. And one was a discreet ad for a prostitute named Doni—if any ad for prostitution can be called discreet. And the number was the same one where I'd left the first message for Doni.

I spent the next half hour on the mindless task of copying Harry's book for Doni without knowing if I'd give it to her. After all, maybe it was the black book that someone had ripped Harry's and my offices apart to find.

Julia had timed storming out with Dillon so she could pick up Jennifer at school—always the practical housekeeper. But I wasn't to get off that lightly, no sir. She dropped the kids off with a curt message that she would talk to me tomorrow about how things had to change around here.

Quite apart from this fight she thought she was having

with me about my suitability as a father, I was glad Julia went home. I wanted to have the children to myself. Even Dillon sensed my mood of circling the wagons—it had now become an emotional as well as a physical reaction. And Jennifer shared my worry about Harry junior. We tried to forget our troubles with several snappy games of Candyland. Then they listened with rapt attention as I read *Charlotte's Web* aloud. But it wasn't long before they deserted me for sleep, a commodity I myself found in short supply. From *Screw* magazine to *Charlotte's Web* all in an afternoon and evening. It was too long a journey.

At four A.M. I found myself standing in front of the refrigerator pouring a glass of milk. I took it into the office and dug into the cache of chocolate chips hidden in the drawer there. I ate the chips and drank the milk, staring at the walls.

What had happened to Harry? Who was after me? How could Carol and Jackie have possibly fallen in love with one another? What could I do about Judy and Harry junior?

There were no answers, but life goes on, and just before eight in the morning I found myself back in the kitchen rustling up some breakfast for Jennifer and Dillon, bug-eyed and having made a simple and utilitarian decision.

I'd simply call Jackie and talk to her. Why not try the direct approach? She could tell me about Carol. All I knew for certain was that Carol said she loved her. Love wasn't always the same from the other person's point of view, was it? Why torture myself when all I had to do was to talk to her?

But what was I going to say about Jackie being a prostitute?

Julia arrived and was as pleased as she could be that I had the kids dressed and fed. Not a word about her anger of the night before. I had recovered about half my fair market value with her by simply getting the kids ready. She took Dillon along as she went off with Jennifer to school. The office phone began to ring just as she went out.

It was Jackie calling me! I felt my heart take a leap as I heard her voice.

"Jay, I need to talk to you. Can I see you tonight?"

I nearly shouted my affirmation into the receiver. We both thought it better if we met somewhere other than my apartment or hers. We agreed on the Balcony Restaurant, at eight o'clock. I didn't try to bring up anything on the phone; it would be soon enough when I saw her.

I started sorting files again and even finished the poor Johnsons' tax return—that's how much more productive I felt. A client of Carol's called and I gave out her number upstairs. Later in the morning I heard Carol pass on her way out. She didn't stop and I didn't try to stop her. There was plenty of time to work out the details of our business and personal separation. It wasn't like we were married. And I didn't feel like speaking to Carol until I'd seen Jackie.

I submerged myself in my work until the doorbell rang just after noon. I was surprised to see Doni standing at the door. She was dressed in a white linen suit and a white blouse with embroidered frills. To complete the image she wore a large black bow tie and had her glasses on again. Her frizzy brown hair was now pulled up in back and controlled by a black comb. But she wouldn't give in to the legal world on the bracelets or the earrings. Her standing there made me remember that she was picking up Harry's black book.

"I'm sorry I can't stay to talk," she said as I let her in. "I'm just on a lunch break and have to get back."

I bit my tongue and didn't ask her what kind of work she had to get back to. I slipped her copy into an envelope and gave it to her, hoping I wasn't cutting my own throat. She promised to get back to me with what she found in the book. I saw her out the door.

Did I feel any attraction for her after our tête-à-tête of the prior afternoon? You bet I did. But I had to sort out the rest of it. Jackie was on my mind. Maybe I would get back to Doni when things settled down.

By evening, Julia was her normal self—after I gave her a groveling apology and explanation of the *Screws* in the office. In fact, she stayed the night with the children.

I made it to the Balcony by a quarter to eight. I brought along another copy I'd made of Harry's little book. Jackie was already there, seated at a table in the back. She was taking no risk of Judy Sage or anybody else interrupting us, which was just fine with me.

She wore a white jumpsuit that had a zipper all the way down the front. The zipper was open far enough to make me imagine pulling it down the rest of the way. The only jewelry she had on was round silver earrings with a design of small glittering stones.

The silver went with her eyes. She looked at me steadily, searching from eye to eye.

I reached over and squeezed her hand. She squeezed back and wouldn't let go. But with my free hand I laid the envelope with Harry's book in front of her. She looked across at me, her eyes now filled with a question, her eyebrows raised slightly.

I had to look down at the table before I could speak. "A copy of Harry's black book of addresses."

I looked up and she still had the brows arched with a question. She nodded to me to continue, a little movement of her chin like someone afraid of what's coming next. Her fingertips just brushed along the top of the envelope.

"You're in it. . . . " I stopped and looked into her silver eyes. " . . . because you're a prostitute."

The eyebrows went down, removing the question mark from her face. She stared blankly at me now, without recognition, like a deer staring into the headlights of an oncoming car. Then her eyes were on mine again.

"Jay, I'm not going to lie to you. I respect you too much. Sure, I made money that way. But it's finished now and it didn't mean anything."

She paused, but didn't take her eyes off mine. More than half of me wanted to reach across the table and grab hold and hang on. To tell her anything was okay with me.

"I could have made money typing manuscripts. But this was a hell of a lot easier and I didn't even have to think." I could see her huffing up a bit. "I suppose you'd rather I had staggered along as a waitress. Saved myself to be dependent on someone like you. Instead, I made fifty thousand a year. What's the difference except that I almost made big, big money?"

I didn't understand her. "What do you mean, 'almost made'?" I asked, puzzled.

She ignored me, she was so intent on what she was saying. "But I'm through with it now. It's too goddamn bitter."

"How long did you do it?"

"What do you want to get at, Jay? The whore is more innocent if she did it less? Is there a little virgin left for you? No there isn't, Jay. There's just a woman putting a normal life back together. If I want to forget anything, I want to forget that I made love to men and it didn't mean a goddamn thing."

She reached into the envelope and pulled out the copy of Harry's black book.

She looked down at it, flipped through the pages once. "Shit, one of these women killed Harry, you can bet on it. One that couldn't get out of it."

I shrugged. What could I say? She brought her eyes back to mine, those silver eyes, watching for my reaction as closely as she could. Then she gave me a soft smile showing me her little teeth—the teeth that gave her away in the *Screw* ad.

"One that couldn't get out of it," she repeated.

Something snapped in me at that.

"Did you get out of it?" My voice was loud enough that we both looked around to see if we were drawing any attention. Except for the few stares from men Jackie always got, we weren't. I reached into a pocket and pulled out the clipping of her *Screw* ad and pushed it across in front of her. "You're talking a good line. But look at this. You see your picture and the number below it?"

Jackie blanched. It was some moments before she could speak. I went forward in the silence.

"Your voice on a tape at this number is still asking men

to leave a message and you'll give them a discreet call."

"Jesus," she said when she'd found her voice, "those bitches are still using my tape." She picked up the ad and walked to the pay phone by the bar. I watched her put in a quarter and dial a number. She listened and then hung up and returned to our table. It was a good act or it was for real.

"You're right about the tape," she said, "but . . . " Then she turned things around one more time. "Let's say I was. What the hell difference should it make to you how I use my body? Whose property is it, anyway? You trying to stake it out as yours?"

"No! Yes! No!" I burst out. She was looking into my eyes and had taken hold of my arm above the wrist and was shaking me. I had to lower my voice consciously before I could continue. "Do you think I could accept sharing a sexual experience with you, if I knew the same thing was happening with forty other guys every week?"

I stopped and rubbed a hand over my eyes to see if I was crying. I wasn't, but I felt like it.

"Look," I said very softly and right into her eyes, "I have to work out this Harry thing. I don't know. Maybe I'm emotionally vulnerable because everything is so off balance. What about you and Carol? What about you and me? I don't want you to answer that, not yet. I'm not looking for answers except to who killed Harry."

She reached for my hand and squeezed it. I appreciated the gesture.

"So," she said as quietly, "who killed Harry?"

I took my hand out of hers and picked up her copy of Harry's book and laid it right on top of the *Screw* ad in front of her.

"Like you said, one of the women listed here."

She picked up the book and thumbed through the pages again, obviously stopping briefly at the *J* section.

"I'm in here," she said so softly that at first I wasn't sure she had spoken.

"Yes, you are."

"Have you talked to all these women?"

"No. They don't much like talking to strangers. They'll agree to get you off but to talk about themselves or anybody who might be named Harry is forbidden. Aside from yourself and another woman named Doni, only Melissa was willing to talk. Melissa is dead. She was murdered because . . ." I had to stop. I didn't know why she was murdered.

I had been right. It was easier to talk about murder and prostitution than it was to talk about love and love triangles. I changed gears and came straight at Jackie.

"Carol says she's in love with you."

She looked at me, again arching her eyebrows with a question. But she was not afraid to look into my eyes.

"Did she?" she said softly.

"And I love you too," I said, the admission catching in my throat.

She didn't blink and her eyes searched into mine. She reached out and held my hand.

"You barely know me."

I laughed for the first time. "It's tough enough to be in love with you. Do I have to know you too?"

She laughed at me and I loved her more.

"Well, I have some news for you."

I waited and I'm sure she could feel my hand tense up in hers.

"You don't have to worry about that," she said. "I love you too, Jay. There's no choice between you and Carol. I want to be with you."

I felt a soaring confidence return. She loved me and let Carol be damned. I felt myself breaking into a big smile.

"I'd convinced myself that I'd never see you again," I told her.

She smiled too. "I thought I'd screwed it up for good too. I wanted so badly to call you. I just didn't know how I'd be received. My heart sank when I came down those stairs and saw you standing in the hall. I have to tell you how it happened."

I reached over and ran the tips of my fingers down her face and into her mouth. She kissed at them while keeping her eyes looking into mine.

"Don't tell me now," I said. "You've told me too much."

She rose from the table, pulling me up by the hand she held. "Enough telling, let's go."

Jackie didn't get any arguments from me. And it was lucky for the City of New York that her apartment was close by.

Her bed was piled high with pillows and a light blue comforter. And I liked the bed because it was still mussed up and unmade. She put on some Thelonius Monk.

Jackie offered me champagne and I popped the cork and poured us each a glass. Then we sat together on the bed facing her window overlooking Riverside Park and the Hudson. A full moon caught the river and the sparkling light covered us. I kissed her for a while and we took off each other's clothes. And we made love. This time it felt like I'd done it with her for years and as if it were the first time.

In the very middle, Jackie looked at me, looked right into my eyes. "Is this really happening?"

And I knew what she meant. Not that we were making love, not that we were having sex, but that we had fallen hopelessly into one another in that deep way which is an opening to love, compassion.

Jackie whispered into my ear and wrapped herself around me so that my body was inside her and I was inside her too.

Late in the night, after the moon had set, I heard the phone ringing. It felt like it went on ringing for a long time.

▽

18

I ARRIVED HOME EARLY enough to get Dillon and Jennifer up, dressed, and fed before Julia woke up. She was sacked out on the convertible couch in the office. If she had her opinions about me being away overnight she kept them to herself for once, probably mollified by my early arrival. Also, my obvious good spirits helped after having been a grouch for two days. I told Julia to leave the convertible open and that I'd clean up the office. Little did she know that I stretched out on the convertible for a second and was asleep the minute she and the children left.

I'd been asleep about an hour when the phone rang. It was Fran Pappas calling from a pay phone at 103rd and Broadway. Her flat, nasal voice was so loud I had to hold the receiver a foot from the ear she was trying to fill.

"Mr. Jasen. Oh! They were here—I mean at Harry's office. It was so terrible. *She* told me I was fired and to leave the office." Fran was breathless.

"Calm down, Fran. Who was there? What did they say to you?"

"Oh! *That* woman and a man. I don't think I can stand it!" And to prove her point, Fran started to bawl. I wondered if I could get anything rational out of her.

"Easy now, Fran. It will all turn out okay. What was the name of the woman?"

"The name?" She sounded incredulous, as if I were making an accusation. "Uh . . . uh," she said and I couldn't tell if she were catching her breath or starting another crying jag. But it came out as anger.

"Judy Sage," she snapped at me. "Who else could it be."

It wasn't a question and I refrained from getting out Harry's book and reading her the possibilities.

I went on to question her. "I suppose the man was a Korean who couldn't speak English very well?"

"Korean? Yes, somebody from over there, I think. How did you know that?"

"Just a guess."

"Can they fire me, Mr. Jasen?"

"They can't fire you, Fran. You work for me, remember? But they can certainly make you leave Harry's office. I think we will have to be as diplomatic about it as we can. Do you still have the keys?"

"No. They took the keys away from me."

"They took our set too, Fran. So it's not just you. Judy's Moonie advisers are afraid of everyone not under their control. You. Me. Even my kids. But don't worry. As far as I'm concerned, you're still on the payroll."

"I'll come right over to your office, Mr. Jasen. Right now."

"Hmmm," I said. The last thing I needed was Fran breathing down my neck. "Not for the moment. Why don't you just go on home and wait for my call. It's a pity they took your keys."

"Oh, yeah. All I have left is the combination," Fran went on. "I'd forgotten all about the combination until you just mentioned the keys. But it's not to the office anyway and I think even Harry forgot he'd given it to me. Do you think I should call to tell them, Mr. Jasen?"

"It's not to the office," I repeated dumbly.

"No," she said. "Do you think I can go to the police about her, Mr. Jasen? She killed him. Now I know she did."

"Wait, Fran, please call me Jay. And what's this combination of Harry's you have? It's not to the office?"

"Oh. Yes."

"What's it to?" I did a very good job of not screaming at her.

"Oh? Well, it's only a mailbox he had somewhere. The Cathedral Station post office I think."

I waited so that I would be calm and she would be listening for what I was going to say. "Look, Fran, I want you to do me a big personal favor. Do you know what post office box it is?"

"Sure. I have it written right here next to the combination. You want me to tell you?"

"No. Something else."

"Yes, anything you want, what is it?"

"I want you to meet me at the post office. Would you do that for me?"

"Oh, sure, Mr. Jas . . . Jay, but . . . "

"Fran, do you know what's in that mailbox?"

"No. I never went there. Harry did it on his own. I think he forgot he gave me the combination when he hired me."

"How soon can you meet me there, Fran?"

"Oh? Oh. Would fifteen minutes be okay, Mr. Jasen?"

"That'll be just fine. And Fran?"

"Yes, Mr. Jasen?"

"Call me Jay. I mean it, okay?"

"Oh!"

I flew up to the post office. Fran, even though she must have been only a block away, took half an hour to get there. And it wasn't like she fixed herself up. She was breathless as if she had run all the way and her face was still streaked with the tear marks of her little confrontation with Judy and the Moonie.

"Mr. Jasen . . . " she began.

"Jay, Fran, Jay. It's going to be okay." I was happy enough to see her that I gave her a big hug. I was surprised this time. She had on that scent—the one the woman had been wearing in Harry's office the night they attacked me.

"Fran, where did you get that perfume?"

She flushed red, embarrassed. "I'm sorry, Jay. If I did wrong just tell me. Harry had a big box of it. He said he gave it out to clients as gifts. It's called Knowing." She gave me a timid smile. "I didn't think he needed it anymore. I took the box. He had ten bottles left. Do you like it?"

"It's great," I said. But I also knew why everyone I met was wearing Knowing. Harry had passed the perfume out to anyone he'd slept with.

"You have the combination?"

She dipped into her purse and came up with a small piece of paper. I took it from her and went to the box number. Then I followed the combination and the box popped open.

The box contained eleven pieces of mail, all correspondence from the Internal Revenue Service. Five of them were easily recognizable without opening them. Government checks. But I wasn't about to open the envelopes except in the privacy of my own office.

I thanked Fran expansively and sent her home. When I reached my office, no one was there. I was able to sit down at my desk in peace and carefully slice open each envelope. Then I laid the contents out in front of me.

The five checks from the IRS were all made out to Harry Sage. They varied in amounts from a low of $85.00 to a high of $10,560. The letters backed up the checks in a very strange way. Each letter referred to the amount on one of the checks. Then the letter explained that the check was in payment of the Internal Revenue Services' fee of ten percent of the tax collected based on information Harry had provided.

I found myself sagging back into my desk chair and staring at the letters and checks. "Damn!" I said aloud and I slammed my hand down on the desk.

Harry was a bounty hunter!

How simple! He wasn't doing anything illegal like embezzlement or blackmail. He was a legal bounty hunter! He went from prostitute to prostitute, exotic dancer to exotic dancer, trying to get close enough to find out some personal details.

Things like their real names and social security numbers. Then their bank accounts or however else they disposed of the large amounts of cash they pulled in. After that, Harry would write a report to the IRS. And then he'd wait for his ten percent to roll in after the IRS had audited and collected the taxes on the unreported income. And for many of these women, the collection might be for a series of years.

It occurred to me that Harry deducted the money he spent on women like Melissa on his tax return. Fees to prostitutes for services were legal for him as a necessary investigation expense. Deductible sex.

It explained a lot of things. Like what Melissa had put together for me. And hadn't Jackie and Doni said Harry had helped them with the IRS. Helped them with audits he had caused! What a creep Harry was. Harry the snitch. Harry the bounty hunter.

Someone might have taken a real exception to a bounty hunter—especially a victim.

Harry had picked a good city for his little business. The supply of prostitutes and exotic dancers in New York was inexhaustible. And I bet he picked only on women alone or in pairs so that he wouldn't have to deal with the mob. And isolated from one another, they would never figure out what was going on.

But someone did figure it out and didn't like it.

I read each of the IRS letters carefully. Except for the amount and the case reference, they were the same. And all signed by a special agent, Thomas Lewis.

I knew one of the targets. Judith Steinberg's audit resulted in a check of $716.85 to Harry. Judith Steinberg was Doni and she must be paying the IRS a tax bill of $7,168.50 if the ten percent collection rule held.

The check for $10,560 was the only one for which a letter of explanation had not arrived yet. But I could imagine the staggering tax bill on that one—over $105,000. Maybe he'd nailed a madam.

I didn't know any of the other names besides Judith

Steinberg. I did check Harry's black book, but none of them were in there. Of course, that would be true because the women all used other identities in prostitution.

Doni was the only link I had between the bounty-producing audits and the women in the book. Maybe she'd have an idea on how to find the murderer. But she had thought Harry was her lover. Had she found out about this and become so angry with Harry she'd killed him? But for $7,000? No, not for $7,000. But for doing that to her? Possibly? I'd think about killing a lover if she'd done that to me.

Hey, okay, say Doni did kill him for betraying her. Then why would she try to kill me? Or Melissa? It didn't make sense, even if I was Harry's partner in a bounty-hunting enterprise.

I remembered Harry had said he needed a partner who knew his way around the IRS. And I could see what he meant about getting a lot of women. I just wished I could talk the whole thing over with Carol. She would be a good head to get in on this. But since I wasn't talking to Carol, I decided to take Doni. If she knew all this, maybe she could put the rest of it together. Maybe I could convince her that Harry operated on his own and I wasn't the bastard he was.

I called Doni at her apartment but got no answer. I called the number on the business card she'd given me and left a message on an answering machine.

Jackie was the next person I tried. She may not have had her name on one of the letters describing checks, but she could easily give me some more information if I told her what had happened. But there was no answer and no machine at her number.

I worked through the afternoon, calling Doni and Jackie about every fifteen minutes without reaching either of them. After the second hour of the attempt, I added Carol to my list. But I had no luck with her either. Then about five o'clock, I heard Carol coming in through the foyer. I opened my door and called to her as she climbed the stairs.

She came back slowly, reluctant to get into a conversation. But I told her what had happened with Fran and the post office box. Then I showed her the IRS letters and checks. She jumped to all the same conclusions I had.

"I think you should head over to Doni's place now," Carol advised. "It's a mistake to wait here, hoping she might call. She's the only real name we can identify. She could give you the real dope on this."

I found myself nodding with her, happy she was there telling me what to do. "I'll go, if you can hang out here. Either Doni or Jackie might call."

"Sure," Carol said, "just let me run up and put my phone on call forwarding. After all, it's more likely Jackie will call there than here."

I wasn't about to start an argument with Carol or break the news to her as to where Jackie said her true feelings lay. I nodded and waited until she got back.

It took twenty minutes to get across town to Doni's place in the East Sixties and it must have been about six o'clock. She didn't have a doorman building and no one was answering the doorbell. I followed another tenant into the building, a teenager, and went up to Doni's door.

The door was open about an eighth of an inch. I rang the bell with no result. Then I pushed the door open a foot and shouted inside. No one responded. It opened onto her living room. I pictured myself taking a quick look around and leaving, maybe uncovering evidence making Doni the murderess. There was an inviting desk right on the other side of the living room.

"Hello, Doni," I shouted. I crossed quickly to the desk. I opened several drawers but found nothing. Not even innocuous letters to a mother or bills to the electric company. I quickly walked down the hallway to the one bedroom. As I did I passed the bathroom where I had changed my wet clothes the day before. I don't know why, but I glanced back over my shoulder as I passed the bathroom door. The angle was right so that I could see someone in the tub reflected in the full-length mirror on the open door. I caught my breath as I turned to run from the apartment. But I had to look in again, this time directly, as I went back down the hall.

She was stretched out in the tub of water. And it was turning slowly red with the blood draining from her wrists. I went in. She looked dead to me. And she had nothing on but the bracelets and earrings. I put a hand on her breastbone so that a finger lay alongside the artery of her neck. I felt a slight beat of the artery.

Quickly I pulled her up so that she wouldn't sink under the water. I grabbed her blouse and underwear from the floor and fashioned tourniquets for her wrists. Then I ran to the phone and dialed 911. This time I correctly gave the operator my name and told her where Doni lived. I didn't give a damn anymore if they pulled me in for Harry's murder or not. Doni must have figured out what had happened. She could have used the black book and known who the murderer was. Then had she confronted that person with her suspicions? And why?

I lifted her out of the tub. As I turned I saw myself in the full-length mirror. My wide midwestern face was as white as a sheet, the brown eyes wild and determined. And I saw myself with the nude, unconscious woman in my arms. I laid her on her bed, drying her carefully with a towel and then covering her with a quilt. With her face drained of blood, her full lips and the slight puffiness under her eyes made her look close to death instead of sensuous.

Holding her as I carried her to the bed, naked and vulnerable looking, made me think of another woman—Jackie. If this had happened to Doni with Harry's book, Jackie was also in danger. And I had given them the book, stupid me! I couldn't let Jackie stay in that kind of danger. She had been unavailable all day too. I pictured her also slowly bleeding to death in her own tub. I had to get out of Doni's apartment. I had to get to Jackie's as fast as I could.

A moment later I was pushing the doorbells on the other apartments on the floor. As luck would have it, the first to answer was a competent-looking little old lady, nosy but helpful. I told her that Judith Steinberg had had an accident and that the EMS ambulance and the police were on the way. I gestured toward Doni's open door as I spoke. Then I ran with her staring after me. There was no way I would be a mistaken identity this time—especially after I'd given my real name to the 911 operator.

I had stopped the bleeding and the little old lady would get them to the right apartment.

EMS and the police were pulling up as I came out and I held the door open. They brushed past me and into the elevator.

I flagged down a cab and told the driver I'd double the fare if he could get me to Riverside at 114th in ten minutes. Was I too late?

I hadn't called Carol. First, I was in a hurry. Second, I didn't want Carol to know I was on my way to Jackie's. It took being thrown back and forth in the speeding cab to figure out I had to call Carol. Perhaps Jackie had checked in and my mission was a foolish and ill-advised one. And, to be fair to Carol, I had to tell her where I was and what had happened. Couldn't Carol also be in danger? At least once I was on the West Side it would be hard for Carol to argue against my going to Jackie's. By the time I reached upper Broadway I had calmed down quite a bit and I had the cabbie drop me at the Silver Bar Café.

I rushed in to the pay phone.

Frederik was there practicing alone on the bowling machine.

"Jay," he called as he saw me heading for the phone. "You ever played this game?" I could see him turning to the bar to get me a drink.

"Not now, Frederik," I shouted back at him.

He came over to me as I was dialing.

"Just one quick one, okay, Jay?"

I shook my head as I waited for Carol to answer.

"You hear from Jackie?" I said when I heard her voice.

She hadn't.

"Someone tried to murder Doni. Slit her wrists and left her to die by bleeding to death or drowning. She was in the bathtub—just like Melissa."

Frederik's black eyebrows narrowed in astonishment as he listened in.

"I'm at the Silver Bar now. I'm going on over to Jackie's."

Carol wanted to come too but my strategy worked. "I'm right here," I told her, "and I can call you when I find her. You come and no one will be there to get her call."

She agreed.

For once in his life, Frederik dropped out of a bowling game. I could tell, though, that he had spent the afternoon drinking.

"Jay, what's all this talk about murder and bleeding to death?"

I put a hand on Frederik's shoulder. "It's true. You heard about Harry Sage's murder. Well, there's a lot of stuff coming down from that. I've got to go, Frederik. I've got to get up to a woman's apartment, she might be in trouble. And she's my lover."

Frederik might not be there when you need him, but when he is, he's got a heart of gold.

"I'm going with you, Jay," he said. And I knew from the tone in his voice and what we'd been through together that he was neither asking me nor would he be put off. And his offer was fine with me. Things were getting deep enough that I'd take the help of anyone at all. Even a friend with one too many drinks in him might be useful. He went to the bar and downed a shot glass of something and then he followed me out.

It was still light outside at that time in May. We walked rapidly over to Riverside Drive and up to 114th Street. I walked fast and Frederik did the best he could to keep up.

"This girlfriend the one you met the night we went with Harry?" Frederik asked me.

I turned to scowl at him for his drunken forgetfulness.

"What're you talking about? We never met any women with Harry."

Frederik was quiet trying to keep up with me.

"Then what about two weeks ago?" he said. He stopped behind me and I rushed on. I didn't know what he was talking about.

"Yeah," he shouted at my back, "that guy Harry. Where'd you find him?"

I turned on him. He was about twenty feet behind now. "Harry's dead," I said, trying to cut him off and get him moving.

"Dead?" he repeated, narrowing his black eyebrows at me and licking his lips in the middle of his gray-streaked black beard. "Boy, that's right. You didn't stay that night. It was Harry. Harry took Chinless and me to the women."

Frederik got me with that. I moved back toward him, torn now between what he had to say and getting to Jackie's.

"What happened?" I asked.

"Well, Harry owed Chinless and me a lot of money. After you left we kept popping him for double or nothing." Flash shook his head unbelieving. "I was so loaded it's lucky I remember anything. Harry said he'd give us our money's worth in great lays. Hell, Chinless winked at me and said it sounded good. Harry made a phone call. Then took us in a cab.

"Oh boy, what a time we had, Jay. Harry had this lady with the greatest eyes. She'd brought in the others for Chinless and me. Two each. I left and took one home with me." He shook his head. "She was something, Jay."

I turned away from Frederik, disgusted with Harry and his life and prostitutes, and with Frederik too. Harry got all the women he wanted and screwed them all, first in bed, later with the IRS. I left Frederik and hurried on toward Jackie's building. He fell in behind me again. He continued to talk at my back.

"Chinless got drunk the other night. Said he's in love with Harry's old girlfriend. Hard to believe, a beautiful woman like that."

I was barely listening to him anymore. And I was tired of finding Harry's women. I turned and cut him off because we had arrived at Jackie's building. I told him to wait and I pointed up to the building. "I'll be in the eighth-floor apartment on the corner. I'll yell down to you. Keep your eyes open."

Frederik stopped talking and nodded.

I didn't want Frederik taking a drunken version of what Jackie and I said to one another to spread at the Silver Bar Café.

There was no doorman in the lobby. I pressed her lobby buzzer several long rings. To my surprise, I got an answering buzz. Then it seemed to take forever for the elevator to arrive and slowly rise to the eighth floor. As I stepped off the elevator the big guy I'd encountered in Harry's apartment came rushing around the hall corner. I ducked, but he wasn't looking for me. He pushed past into the elevator. In a moment the door had closed and the car had started downward.

But I was running along the hall. The door to Jackie's apartment stood wide open. I ran through the apartment. No one was there. Then I ran to the window facing Riverside Drive and threw open the sash. Frederik was standing outside on the sidewalk where I'd left him. I saw the big guy running out of the building and now there was a second guy with him.

"Frederik!" I shouted. He looked up, swaying slightly, trying to locate me. Then he saw me and waved. "It's them," I shouted pointing down at the two men.

He looked over at them, passing right by him, and then up at me.

"But it's only Chinless," he shouted.

I did a double take and saw he was right. It was Chinless. He and the big guy had brushed by Frederik and were getting into a car parked illegally at the bus stop.

"Can't you do something?" I shouted in frustration. If I had thought about it I wouldn't have shouted that. I would have shouted for him to get out of the way. And as soon as

I said it, I was sorry. Myself, I would have run.

Frederik looked up at me one more time, then stepped over in front of their car waving his hands vaguely in the air.

He was tossed up across the trunk of another parked car and my heart came up in my throat. He lay there like a rag doll as the big guy, driving, and Chinless, backed up, did a U-turn, and sped off.

"Jay?" I heard from behind me.

I turned and Jackie was standing there looking at me.

"Oh, God," she said, "I'm so glad it's you." She rushed to me and threw her arms around me. "I heard your voice. I was hiding."

I returned her hug. "It's a long story," I said. "Are you okay?" She nodded at me weakly, looking into my eyes. I broke away and went to the window. "Frederik is down there. He was just hit by their car. I've got to call an ambulance."

I picked up the phone and dialed 911. Jackie, still clutching me, took the phone and gave them the information but she gave them a false name when they asked.

"What's going on?" I asked, frowning at her for her lie.

"It was terrible, Jay. He had a key or something and let himself in. I heard him coming and hid. Under the bed like a little kid would do. He came right into the bedroom looking for something. He even took the paintings off the wall. I'm sure he was searching from the top down. He would have gotten to me under the bed. Then you rang the bell. That scared him. He waited by the door. Then when you kept ringing, he went into the living room. I came out and sneaked into the kitchen and rang the reply buzzer. Then he ran."

"I have to tell you I think I saved your life," I told her. She looked into my eyes and stepped in close and clung to me. I hugged her back. I was so happy she was safe.

"Let's get out of here," I said. "Get some stuff for a day or so. We're going somewhere safe." I went back to the window while she packed up. Frederik hadn't moved but several people had gathered around him now and I could hear a siren in the distance.

By the time Jackie and I got to the street, an ambulance was pulling up. Frederik, now lying on the pavement, was moaning and someone had put a sweater under his head. Jackie and I went to him. He opened his eyes and seemed to recognize me, but looked past me at her.

"It's going to be all right," I said, "don't worry."

"Jay," he said, his voice a hoarse whisper, "the girl Chinless was with—"

The squawk of a police bullhorn cut him off as a squad car arrived. Jackie pulled me back.

"Let's get away," Jackie said. "I'm scared and I don't trust the police. I've been booked too many times. There would be endless questions to answer. He'll be okay. You can't do anything for him now."

She pulled me away and I went. But I also went because I didn't want to give all the explanations. I had reported Doni and now I was at this scene. And I was in big trouble for withholding evidence—even if everything else was explained. And Jackie was right, Frederik was in professional hands.

Jackie and I quickly walked away and across 114th to Broadway. There we got a cab to the Hertz rental and, bingo, I had her in a car and on the Long Island Expressway on the way to the Peconic Bay house.

I'd killed two birds with one stone. I'd not only gotten Jackie away but I was taking her to my favorite place.

As I drove, she looked at me, questioning me with those silver eyes of hers. "Now tell me, what's going on."

"It's Harry and that damn book of his. Every one of us who has it is in danger. I don't mean to startle you. Harry had another lover. A woman named Doni. She also had a copy of the address book and I found her bleeding to death this afternoon. That's why I came over to your apartment. And just in time. You were next."

Jackie's eyes opened wide. "Another lover? I wish I'd never met Harry." She stopped to reflect before she continued. "But how did they know I had Harry's book?"

I shook my head. "Did you look it over?"

Jackie nodded. "It didn't make any sense to me. What was it about?"

I told her about Harry's game: Harry the IRS bounty hunter. Jackie shuddered as if freezing. I reached over and she gripped my hand with both of hers.

"I don't know where I'd be without you, Jay."

When we got off the Long Island Expressway, I stopped at a gas station and called Carol from a pay phone. When I told her that Jackie was with me and we were on our way to the Peconic Bay house she hung up on me.

She did pick up when I called back. I begged her to listen. She said she would but only for a minute. Then I told her what had happened at Jackie's and why we were fleeing the city.

"What should we do now?" I asked.

"I'll tell you what, I think we ought to get Scarf in on the whole story."

I thought about that. "It's a good idea. What do you think about asking him to come to the Peconic Bay house? That way I can convince Jackie to give her version of the story. And we're safe there."

Carol liked the idea. She said she'd get hold of Scarf as soon as possible. Now that we were crying for his professional help, I didn't see any problem convincing him to pay us a visit.

"Just tell him we want to talk to him alone first." When I got back into the car, Jackie asked me who I'd called. I told her I was just checking in with Carol and she seemed satisfied. I didn't see any point in telling her about Scarf yet.

▽

19

IF IT WEREN'T FOR the dead and the wounded scattered along the way, I was now in the perfect place to be. I was with the woman I loved at a vacation house on an ocean bay. We were alone. And she loved me too.

The apple tree between the road and the house was in full blossom, white in the night. I showed her into the house. The picture windows gave her the view of the Peconic Bay looking wide under the rising moon. We began to kiss and litter our clothes from the kitchen through the living room into the bedroom until there were no more clothes left. Then we were on the bed. We were fast, desperate, furious.

When we were lying quiet again and I was petting her face, I told her that Scarf was on his way out and I had decided we should tell him everything we knew about Harry and his bounty hunting. She was suddenly very angry. She jumped up from the bed and stood there, naked, her hands on her hips.

"I suppose you told him I'm a whore," she shouted at me. "If you get me convicted of prostitution, Jay, what do you think that will do to my future? You think I'm going to sacrifice a chance at a straight life to catch some lousy killer who does away with hookers and bounty hunters?"

I hadn't thought about it from her point of view. "Carol told Scarf to meet us here. He doesn't have to know exactly who you are, let's just tell him you also knew Harry. It's up to you what you want to say after that."

"Shit!" she said, and stalked off to the bathroom. She let me stew for about five minutes, but when she came back, she seemed to have worked it out for herself. She was very much calmer.

I showed her around the house. In the kitchen, I pointed out Harry's revolver I'd left wrapped in the sweater on top of the refrigerator. She said it made her feel safer.

That's when I picked up the kitchen phone to call Carol. But Jackie put a hand on top of mine.

"Don't call yet," she said. "Let's leave the outside world where it is for a few more minutes."

This time we made love with deliberation. I wanted to be with her forever. She made me go slowly, stopping and going on again.

"Whatever happens, Jay," she whispered into my ear between little gasps and nips, "I love you."

Once, when we were resting, I asked, "Are you sure it's me you really love?"

She looked perplexed.

"Me, not Carol?"

"I want the love and trust of a man. I trust you, Jay."

"I love you," I said.

"Do you trust me?"

I nodded that I did and placed my head on her breasts like a child in her arms.

I did feel secure there, and after the draining day and with the quiet of the country house, I went to sleep.

I awoke a little while later and I was alone in the dark. I heard Jackie walking in bare feet from the kitchen to the bedroom. She wore an old floppy shirt of mine and was carrying two glasses of scotch with ice. She sat on the edge of the bed and handed me one. Then she toasted.

"To us."

We touched the glasses and drank.

"We have some protection," Jackie then said.

"What do you mean?"

"There's a cop out back on the road. He says Scarf sent him to keep an eye out for us until he gets here."

I felt very relieved. I got up and pulled on some trousers. Then I went into the kitchen and looked out the back window onto a moonlit lawn broken by the dark shadows of the trees. There was a car parked in the shadows across the road from the house. I could make out the form of a man sitting in it and the glow of his cigarette.

"I'm going out to see if he knows when Scarf is due," I said. I flicked on the porch light and went out, walking slowly across the street to the car.

The cop stayed inside, his face hidden, but I could see he wore a policeman's cap. Only his arm on the window, bare because he had the sleeve rolled up, and the glow of his cigarette were visible.

"Scarf send you?" I asked him.

"Yeah," he said, "Officer Grazzio. Bruce asked me to keep everything under wraps until he gets here."

He pulled out a badge in a little leather folder and held it out the window for me to examine. There was enough light from the porch when he held it out the window to see his picture and name next to the badge.

"It's very informal," he went on, "this isn't our jurisdiction."

But when he held up the badge, he also exposed the bare skin of his arm above the wrist. I could see the clear evidence of four long scratches down his arm. I stopped, trying to connect the scratches with a memory. A cat's claws had gotten hold and held on.

"Great," was all I could manage, "really great."

I backed away from him, hoping I looked casual and in control. Then I turned my back and walked slowly to the house, feeling that a bullet could rip into me at any second.

"Oh God, oh God, oh God," I said as I came through the door.

"What's wrong, Jay?"

"That guy may be a cop," I said, "but he's not on our side. He may even have killed Harry. He busted a flashlight over my head the night of Harry's murder."

I grabbed the phone but there was no dial tone. "The phone's dead."

"What are we going to do? You have any neighbors?"

"At this time of year? No. There's a house around the point where the Sterns retired. It's nearly a half mile. The other houses are shut up until summer.

"Damn it," I went on. I was wired now. I took the gun down from the fridge and jammed it into my belt behind my back. Then I turned out the kitchen light and peered over to where our "protector" sat calmly smoking his cigarette.

"What are we going to do?" Jackie said, peering out over my shoulder.

I shook my head. "That's how he got out of my apartment before the police got there. He had somebody listening in on their calls. This must be a big deal Harry had going if rogue cops are involved."

We both sat at the kitchen table where we could see him sitting in the car across the road. Jackie got out a cigarette and lit up. If he made a move, we'd know it.

Then Scarf pulled into the yard, stopping near the apple tree. As he got out, the other guy left his car and approached Scarf. I went to the door and opened it, shouting at Scarf. He just moved toward me, big and black and grinning, thinking I was greeting him with some funny deal. And the other guy moved up quickly so he was only a step behind as Scarf reached the porch.

"How you feeling today, Jay?" Scarf said, a broad smile on his face. He wore a black leather jacket and held out his hand to take mine but it never made it. I knew the other guy now. I'd seen him in Harry's office and at the Little League game. Black hair and black mustache.

"Watch out,' I tried to shout. But even as I did, Scarf was crashing to the floor. I saw the reversed pistol in the guy's hand, the butt having just landed hard on the back of Scarf's head. Bruce tried to get up, crawling crablike along the floor into the kitchen, shaking his head, dazed. The cop hit him again. Behind me I heard Jackie give a little squeal of surprise.

Scarf's fall had forced me back a step. I reached behind me and grabbed Harry's revolver, pulling it up and leveling it at the big guy and not waving it as I had the last time he'd come charging at me in Harry's office. His own weapon was still held butt forward.

He frowned at me.

"What the hell's going on?" he growled. And he just stood there surprised, not dropping the gun but not moving to shoot me with it either, still holding it butt forward. I glanced down at Scarf. He wasn't moving. I saw a red mat of blood forming in his hair. It began to leave a dark red pool on the floor.

Jackie was standing just behind me. "Careful, Jay," she said, "I don't think it's loaded."

"Sure it's loaded," I said. I didn't even look at it. "I loaded it myself when I took it out of Harry's drawer."

I looked sideways at her. She had her eyes closed and was shaking her head in little violent twists. Her floppy shirt was open and I thought she looked too sexy. One caressing little hand was held out towards me, open. On the palm I saw the cartridges and knew all five were there without counting them.

But I turned the gun up so that I could look into the chambers. Empty. The big guy was on top of me before I had time to look at him again. One hand grabbed my right arm at the wrist, forcing the gun down, and the other cracked the butt end of his revolver against my chin hard, snapping my head back against the doorjamb behind me. He had my gun and his gun and stepped back, getting his loaded one leveled on me quickly. I tasted blood in my mouth.

I looked around at Jackie. Wouldn't she close that goddamn floppy shirt of hers? Her face had gone dead white under the tan. She smiled a weak smile. "I'm sorry. I took them out because I didn't want anybody to get hurt."

"Shut up," the big guy shouted. "You," he gestured at me with his pistol, "lie on the floor on your stomach." I did as he said. He used handcuffs to attach my wrists to the kitchen radiator. Then he took Jackie and they went out. I tried calling to Bruce, but he was out cold. When they came back, he had some nylon sailing rope, the kind that doesn't stretch much, and a bunch of coat hangers. He made Jackie lie face down on the floor and I didn't much like the way he touched her when he did it. Then he used some nastily twisted coat hangers and bound up Scarf and me head to foot. That was added to putting my cuffed hands behind my back for me. Scarf's cuffs were used the same way on him although poor Bruce seemed to be in pretty bad shape. He made Jackie help him drag us across the floor and into the middle bedroom. The bastard put out the lights and closed the door on us.

Scarf never woke up.

"You catch some shut-eye until we're ready for you," the big guy shouted as he closed the door. With the shades down, it was very dark. I had enough adrenaline going through me that neither my chin nor the back of my head hurt much yet.

I strained my ears to hear what was happening. I heard them moving into the front bedroom facing the water. I had been making love to her there less than an hour before.

"Stop it," I heard her shout. There was a scuffle and I heard Jackie sobbing. I listened, trying not to breathe, trying to hear everything I could. But then I was listening to my own frightened breathing and Bruce's labored gasping. The silence was more unbearable than the sounds they made and I wished I could hear them again.

I pulled and twisted at my bindings. Forget wriggling out or cutting through with a sharp fingernail. The rope went around my neck and back to the ankles which were doubled up and felt like they wouldn't come any further up my back, then the wrists cuffed and bound to the ankle-neck rope behind me so that pulling on anything choked me. Twisted coat hangers were thrown in here and there just for the fun of it.

I wasn't going anywhere.

I couldn't see how Scarf would fare any better—if he ever woke up to try.

Then I thought of Scarf's little nickel-plated revolver in the ankle holster. I rolled over and, ignoring the pain, twisted around so that I could get at the holster. It was empty. We had no options.

What this big guy didn't know was that the wall between the middle bedroom and the living room was paper thin. I heard someone walking around the living room. Then he went outside. A long time passed. When he came back I could hear two sets of footsteps. The big guy sat on the couch along the other side of the bedroom wall. It was like he was in the room.

"Sounds good," he said. "Two old buddies in a boating accident."

Somebody answered him from a distance and I could tell it was a woman's voice.

He spoke again. "But you gotta get the water in their lungs. Nobody's going to believe they got drowned if there's no water in the lungs. Knock them out and the doctor finds blows to both heads and maybe not enough water in the lungs. But you don't knock them out and maybe one of them swims away. And it don't look like an accident if they're all tied up."

The woman said something.

"That's a great idea. Sure. In the bathtub, then take them out and sink the rowboat." He chuckled.

There was quiet for a moment. Would they be drowning all of us, Jackie too? I was shaking. I didn't want to die.

"I'll get it out of the way now," the big guy said.

I heard someone walk into the bathroom and start the water running into the tub. It was terrifying to listen to that water running. And it blocked out hearing anything else they said. When it stopped, the dying would start.

I struggled around a little bit and succeeded in getting some telltale rope burns on my neck. Perhaps if I struggled violently enough I would strangle myself and then the medical examiner would catch them out because I'd have no water in my lungs. That made me think of something else—another mistake they were making. I remembered *Chinatown* where the husband had died in the ocean with fresh water in his lungs.

The running water was turned off and I heard a swirl of the water like when one tests the temperature of a bath. Would it just be cold water? Would it be comfortably tepid?

Just then the bedroom door opened and the light came on. I looked up as best I could and saw the big guy standing there over us. He didn't seem particularly cruel. Just businesslike.

"Okay," he said, "who wants to be the brave one?"

"Scarf's still out," I said stupidly, "I think you might have killed him."

He was worried for a moment. It would defeat his plan if he couldn't drown Scarf. But he bent over Bruce and I could see him put his fingers alongside Scarf's throat.

"He's alive, all right. For now, anyway." He paused. "Well, you go first, smart guy." He grabbed my shirt at both shoulders and pulled me along like a sack of potatoes. And, hey, I confess. I wet my pants. But I don't think he even noticed. I forgot them immediately myself. Just as soon as he had heaved me up and over into the tub. Everything was wet then and I was lying on my stomach, all of me under water but my feet and head. I still managed to hold my head up by arching my back as much as I could and pulling at my neck with the rope tied from my neck to my ankles. The water was warm. I felt the pressure of his hand beginning to force my head down and under and I knew that once he had it under the water I would never say anything again. It was at that moment that I played my last card.

"I have some advice for you," I shouted.

"What?"

The pressure of his hand on my head let up just a little, letting my head stay up until he heard what I had to say. Then that was going to be it.

"Shouldn't you be doing this in ocean water? In salt-water?"

"What?"

"Seawater. I heard you talking. How can you get away with them thinking we drowned if we have fresh water in our lungs?"

"Jesus," he said. He let go of my head and left me there in the bathtub. And even without him it wasn't easy to hold my head above the bathwater with my hands tied to my ankles behind my back. I did a little better by rolling to one side.

But I was on my own for only the briefest of minutes. He was soon back and he pulled the plug without a word of thanks or anything. For my part, I'd take the fifteen minutes extra of life over gallons of fresh water in my lungs. Right then I thought about the tub drain. We'd always had trouble with it, what with all the guests and kids tracking sand into the house from the beach. The plumber was supposed to have come around to fix it. This was my first chance to see if he had. True to local form, he hadn't. The water would take forever to drain out. The big guy began to curse when he saw how slowly the water level was going down. I definitely got the feeling he wanted the whole thing over with.

"Come on," I told him on one of his visits to check the water level, "give it up. Why kill us? Somebody's going to track you down, anyway. They can't pin the other stuff on you. Why take a chance with us? Give us a break?"

He responded by pushing my nose down hard through the ten inches of remaining water into the porcelain bottom of the tub, making my eyes fill with tears and causing me to choke so that I couldn't talk. It was a taste of what was to come.

He left again and came back with one of the children's sand pails. He used it to bail the water into the toilet. He helped the tub along until there was just an inch of water beneath me. I was, more or less, relaxing my back and neck muscles from the strain of holding up my head. He suddenly came in carrying a big yellow plastic garbage pail—the solid one we used in the kitchen. And he dumped it, cold seawater, all over me. He left and I began to shiver. Fear and cold is a good mixture to produce a shiver. My jaw hurt. The rope hurt. My nose hurt. He came back with another bucket. The bathtub filled at an alarming rate. I could taste the salt. A tiny hermit crab swam just beneath my nose. He would have something good to eat soon. I twisted to get a good look at the big guy's black mustache and full head of hair—very prominent eyebrows. He frowned as he dumped another garbage pailful onto me. And then he came again. I gave him two more times at most. The saltwater, freezing, was up high around my shoulder even when I rolled onto one side. I was having real trouble keeping my head up. I began to think about not seeing Jennifer or Dillon ever again. That was what I regretted most. Why did he have to kill me?

He put that big hand on top of my head. I really wanted to get a deep breath. I had once seen a film where the character had fooled a murderer pretending to have drowned, holding his breath. But I found myself sobbing out, crying with my own sorrow at the children's loss. Again orphaned. I tried to shout out of my sobbing, to stop him, to reason with him.

He didn't go for it.

I struggled for a minute under the water. Then I pretended to be dead for a minute, maybe a minute and a half. He didn't buy that either. My fake bubbles were all gone. Then the real ones were going out of my lungs and the water, real seawater, was coming in. I couldn't get any air. That was it. I struggled for all I was worth—for Dillon, for Jennifer, for Jackie, for Carol. But he was pulling my legs up over my back so that I wouldn't break my own neck in the fight for my life. Then it felt like he had decided to sit on me to hold me under. The last thing I remember in this life was an explosion in my head.

▽

20

IF HEAVEN IS GETTING French-kissed by Carol, then I was in heaven. She had her mouth tightly over mine, but I realized she wasn't using her tongue. She seemed to be trying to force her lungs into mine. All I wanted to do was to throw up. I choked and rolled away from her, letting water come out of my mouth and onto the floor. My hands and ankles were still bound but there was nothing around my neck and my legs were straight.

I shook my head as more water came gurgling out. Carol was cutting at the ankle rope. Then I coughed up more stuff.

"I'm pleased you're alive," she said. It was the kind of understatement she usually made. But she was crying. She cut the rope away from my wrists but they were still cuffed.

"I don't feel pleased," I tried to joke, but my throat wouldn't work yet and it came out as more vomiting of water. I was lying on one side facing into the bathroom. There was a lot of blood on the bathroom floor—I mean like a slaughterhouse—and the big guy was lying right in the middle. Except he didn't have a face anymore. Carol leaned over him, stepping in the mess, searching until she came up with keys. Then she got the cuffs off.

"Scarf dead?" I tried to ask, but it came out " 'Arf 'ead?"

in a retching Carol might have mistaken for another spilling of my guts. But Carol understood and shook her head.

"Scarf's still alive. See that busted window?" She pointed up over the tub. I saw the bathroom window had been smashed. "I had to blow him away right through the glass. He took a bullet in the chest and a second in the face before he called it quits. Otherwise, Jay Jasen, I'd be writing a eulogy for you." She put up a hand and wiped at the tears on one cheek.

" 'ow 'id you know?"

"Later, Jay, later. Scarf's in the middle bedroom. But where's Jackie?"

I shrugged instead of talking.

"Was this guy alone?" Carol asked.

I shook my head and the movement made me toss up some more cookies. "Two of them," I said when I could. "Never saw the other one. Think woman. I heard them walking around. Talking about killing us."

"Nobody here now. Your Hertz rental and another car are out front."

"Scarf's?"

"Probably."

"Isn't Jackie in there?" I nodded toward the front bedroom.

Carol stood up from where she had been rubbing to get the circulation back into my stinging hands and ankles and pushed open the door.

"No," she said. Then she opened the door to the middle bedroom. I sat up gingerly, holding my head with one hand and bracing my back against the wall. We could see Bruce trussed up like a chicken on the floor and out cold.

"He looks so peaceful," Carol sighed. "I suppose I have to cut him loose."

"Carol!" I said. The blood fully rushing to my feet and hands made them feel as if they'd been amputated along the way. Or as if some amateur acupuncturist had gotten loose on them with several thousand misplaced needles. But I also found that I could stand up if I did so carefully.

"I never saw anyone else," Carol told me as she bent over Scarf, cutting away at the rope with a kitchen knife. "When I got here I circled in the shrubbery on the north side. I saw this big black-haired man huffing and puffing, carrying half the ocean inside. Very bizarre. And when he left the house to make one of his trips, I came in the back way. Harry's revolver was on the kitchen table with five loose cartridges. I grabbed it all up and ducked out again before your friend there came back. I loaded up and came around to the bathroom window to see why he was fooling around with all this seawater. Right then he had finished and I saw him pushing you under." She shook her head. "I never thought I could kill anyone, Jay. But I knew it was the only way to save your life. I blasted him with Harry's gun. Two times. It was awful. I couldn't believe it when I had to shoot him a second time. And in the face."

Carol's mouth formed a tight line. "And I was still unlucky. He fell into the tub on top of you. I ran in and pulled him off."

I gave her a jagged smile. "No matter how hopeless it seems, always find an argument to put off your execution."

"What?"

"I'll tell you the story later. How the hell did you get here?"

"I caught the Hampton Jitney. Then hitched in from the Sunrise Highway and walked the rest. Julia has the kids."

"But why?"

"Frederik called me from the hospital. He said he saw a woman Chinless hung around with at the accident. He was worried about you. Next I checked up on Doni. If she knows who tried to kill her, well, that would tell us everything. She's going to be all right. But she won't be talking for another day. Since your phone was out, I thought I better come and make sure you and Jackie were okay."

I took a wobbly step. I felt pretty bad.

"Where's Harry's revolver right now?" I had to say it twice but I was doing better, only choking and coughing a little water.

"Let's see." She had gone back to working on Scarf's bonds and getting him into a more comfortable position with a blanket over him. "Uh, I think it's in the bathroom sink."

Sure enough, she had thrown it into the bathroom sink. I had to step twice in the dead man's blood to get to it. He was lying face down with his head—or what was left of it—twisted sideways, and there was enough blood that he would have drowned in it if he had still been able to breath. I also saw into the bathtub. It was full of red water. And it made me think to look down at my own clothes. I leaned against the wall and threw up again. Then I staggered away into the kitchen and laid the gun back on the kitchen table where Carol had found it. I stripped off my clothes and washed down with paper towels using the liquid soap for dishes. I dumped the paper towels into a big pile on the floor, never using the same one twice. Carol came out and had me steady myself on the edge of the sink while she finished the job. It felt strange, here I was taking all my clothes off with Carol, only to be cared for like a sick puppy. At the end, she carefully washed my face. I sat down and waited until she brought some clean clothes and helped me put them on.

"I got a pillow under Scarf's head. He's really out. I can't tell how badly he's hurt, but his breathing is very fast and shallow. We need a doctor for him, and now."

"I think I can get to the neighbors. It's about a quarter mile around the point. They'll have a phone."

"If they don't scream in terror. Try looking in a mirror."

I tried it. My face was dead white. Also, I had some well-placed contusions under one eye and on my chin and forehead. And along one side of my neck there were still little spots of the big guy's coagulated blood making little dots that the neighbors could connect in Frankensteinlike lines.

"And I'd never know if you got there or not in that condition," Carol said. "You stay here and watch over Bruce. I'll go to the neighbors."

By way of an answer I thankfully fell into a kitchen chair and slumped forward onto my arms. Carol was alarmed.

"If you can't function, Jay, we'll have to think of another tactic. You may have a visitor, you know."

I forced myself to sit up. I saw the gun there and cupped it into my right hand.

"Go," I said. "I'll be just fine."

She saw the determination in my face and left. It was very dark outside and the porch light was off. I could no longer see her once she had gone out the door. My driving to the neighbors would have been faster than her walking. But she was right, I wasn't sure of what I could do and someone had to watch Bruce. Carrying the gun loosely in my hand, I checked up on him. All I could say was he was still breathing. I went back to the kitchen. It occurred to me to turn off the inside lights. Then I opened the windows on three sides so that I could hear anything going on outside. I didn't want anybody gunning me down through the windows like Carol had done to our big friend.

In the quiet night of the country, you can hear a car coming from some distance away. And I heard one. They were coming.

There was enough adrenaline in my blood so I could get to my feet and make it into the backyard. The night outside was bright with the moon overhead. The smell of the apple tree in blossom filled the air. I walked toward the road with no idea of what to do next and the dew made my bare feet wet. My Hertz rental and Scarf's car were both parked side by side but the big guy's car was missing.

The headlights from the approaching car came sweeping up from the left. I stepped into the shadow behind the apple tree before I could be seen. I felt the soft earth of Tiger's new grave between my toes. I was smart enough to close my eyes to protect my night vision. The car pulled up on the lawn and stopped and the lights went out. I opened my eyes and saw Jackie getting out on my side, a man on the other. They came around the front of the car to go toward the house.

The man was shorter than Jackie.

Maybe I should have waited until they were sandwiched

between me and the house. But if the guy dragged Jackie into the house and had Scarf and her as hostages, I'd be out of luck.

I stepped out of the shadow of the apple tree and extended Harry's gun. It should have been clearly visible in the moonlight.

"Don't move. I have Harry's gun."

That, of course, is supposed to do it. I had the drop on the guy and he should have thrown up his hands and said, "Don't shoot. I give up." I didn't count on him being crazy. And he startled me. If he did anything, I thought he'd grab Jackie as a shield.

"Get to the car," he shouted. She confused me more by breaking for the car. He had pulled out a little flat silvery gun. Scarf's pistol. In the moonlight I could see it as clearly as if I was holding it myself.

The flash and explosion of the gun startled me and I ducked as if I could avoid the bullet. He missed.

Jackie was yanking open the car door on the driver's side. I stood up again stupidly. I didn't intend to shoot anyone. Harry's gun now hung loosely in my hand by my side.

"It's me," I shouted. "It's Jay."

His gun flashed and exploded again. I felt something pinch at my right arm.

I had a sense of relief Jackie had gotten away from him. The car lights came on and he was at an angle and they blinded him. But I could see. The trunk of the apple tree shadowed my face. Chinless George! But Chinless always backed down in a fight. What was he doing here standing up like a hero to a man pointing a gun at him? His smile cut across the space between his nose and his nonexistent chin, showing the missing tooth. I raised the gun and squeezed the trigger on Harry's pistol. One shot.

It jumped with the explosion.

Chinless crumpled like a rag doll.

Jackie could see I'd got him. Yet the car backed out fast in reverse, all the way around in a semicircle so Chinless was lost in the dark. But as it backed out an image of Chinless

George jumped into my mind. He was standing at the bar that Friday night and he said, "Kill two birds with one stone. Do my job and get some bucks from him too." And he chuckled to himself all night long as we bowled.

He had been there to watch Harry! Sure, and Jackie was the one pulling his strings. But why had he told her to run and why had he stood up to me? Because he thought she was his woman. His love made this coward into a superman. We had shot at each other for the same reason. And Frederik had known and tried to warn me after he'd been run down but Jackie had pulled me away. Later he warned Carol. Chinless and Jackie. Jackie and Chinless.

"Stop, Jackie," I shouted and I fired Harry's gun into the air.

She threw the car into forward and I aimed at the rear wheels and fired again.

I didn't seem to hit anything. The car roared away.

I limped over to the Hertz rental. The keys were there above the visor where I'd left them. I threw Harry's gun into the little well between the front seats and jumped in. It wasn't fifteen seconds before I was following the red dots of her taillights. The ten-mile run to the Sunrise Highway is straight and open. I could see her lights far away and for the first few minutes it seemed as if I wasn't gaining on her. Then I came up on her rapidly. I could see she was pulling off. She was getting out when I came to a stop behind her. Her car—the big guy's car—sank down toward the right rear. I'd hit the tire.

I left the lights on, shaking as I got out of my car. She was standing against her door, and she was shaking too. She looked toward me, although I'm sure she couldn't see me through the glare of the headlights. Her eyes were silver and sad and I could see her breathing in small gasps through slightly parted lips.

I walked toward her and then she could see me.

"Jay," she cried, "I didn't know. Oh, God, I'm glad it's you."

She ran to meet me and threw her arms around me, burying her head in my shoulder. She was racked with sobs. I pushed her so I could hold her away from me. She stood not touching me. I felt something wet on my arm and looked down. Blood was running down my sleeve from where the bullet had grazed me. I looked back at her.

"Jay. Jay," she cried, "I thought you were the big cop, Grazzio."

I still said nothing. Instead I led her firmly by one arm and walked her around to the other side of the Hertz rental and opened the door for her to get in. I came back and got into the driver's seat, gripping my arm tightly to stop the bleeding.

"Jay," she said softly. I looked toward her and could see her silver eyes, moist and soft. "You and Harry were right. The IRS never found the big money. They just skimmed the top. I should have paid Harry what he wanted. But two hundred grand was a little greedy, don't you think? Why couldn't you get him to go for less?"

"Blackmail?" I was surprised and my voice showed it. "I thought Harry just went after tax bounty? What was this?"

It was her turn to look startled. She stopped and began to cry. "You didn't know what he was doing?"

I shook my head.

"He said you knew everything except who I was. You knew about the coke chain out of Colombia and how we hid the cash and laundered it to reappear. That's why we had to get to you, Jay. Harry said you knew all the facts except who we were."

I shook my head dumbly some more.

"Nothing. That's what I knew."

"See! I just knew you weren't in on it." She gave me a brave smile and her eyes brightened. "You know the IRS got me for over forty-five thousand. But it was nothing. We had big money—me and the others.

"Harry knew the IRS had more money coming and how to tell them about it. But he knew more than money was at stake. It would have put us in prison for years and years. He followed me because I was a call girl but he stumbled onto much more than he had bargained for. And then ten percent wasn't enough for him anymore, not of taxes. No, Harry wanted ten percent of everything we had. He settled for two hundred thousand dollars to look the other way. He said it was you and him that were settling. We'd do it as a buy out of that partnership you had."

She shook her head as if unbelieving and the tears started again.

"Hell, I didn't care, but the big guy, Tony Grazzio, and Chinless too, they didn't like it at all. And Tony had to protect himself as a cop." She had loosened up and there seemed to be nothing she wouldn't tell me. "It wasn't me doing it to Harry and it wasn't you doing it to me. Tony and Chinless killed Harry. Tony and Chinless tried to kill you too. They thought you knew. Not me, I love you, Jay."

She stopped and looked at me, her eyes silver, first looking into one eye, then the other. I licked my dry lips.

"We could blow this place, just you and me," she said very quietly. "I've got more money than you could even imagine. It's time to wrap it up. The bad guys are dead. There's plenty for us. It would be so nice, Jay. It would be so nice."

She looked closely into my eyes. And she reached across and ran her warm fingers up and down the back of my neck and into my hair.

I said nothing but I think she could see the set of my jaw. I started up the car engine but didn't yet put it into gear.

"Jay," she said very softly, not moving her hand, "you may search this wide world over and you'll never find another woman like me."

"God, I hope not." My voice had a hopeless sound to it. "You're the wicked witch. You enchanted Harry and Chinless and Tony. They're dead. And I confess, you got me too. You went after Doni. And I can see that you killed Harry yourself. You enjoyed cutting him up, didn't you? You slit Doni's or Melissa's wrists yourself? Or did you get a man to do those for you?"

She began to slide closer along the seat and then she stopped but didn't remove her hand. I looked down the road away from her.

"All right, fuck you," she said in another voice, another woman. I turned to look at her again, totally surprised when I thought she could never surprise me again. Her lips were parted in a snarl, showing those little teeth I'd first seen in the *Screw* ad, now animal-like. But I was also looking down the barrel of Harry's revolver.

"Turn off the engine."

I did as I was told. My arm had stopped bleeding.

"I tried to save you, Jay. I really tried." Her seductive voice was bitter and had a vicious edge to it I had never heard before.

"You tried!" I shouted at her, my voice shaking without control. "Today you pretended to make love with me, to be gentle and soft because that was what I wanted. Later, big Tony shows up and I hear what I think is a rape going on. But it wasn't. You were just acting out his fantasy like you acted out mine. And maybe you meant to get to me as well as him. I didn't have the real Jackie. He didn't either. Nobody does. I can't run away with you because you're not there to run away with."

Her laugh was more like a cackle. "One thing I can do is fake love. Do you like knowing that what you thought was the real thing was fake, Jay? That you couldn't read it for being fake? Never, never did I give you even a little sliver of the real thing. Never, never. That's what I like doing, acting out a fantasy someone else thinks is real. I like the power of control."

She laughed again and this time it was near hysteria.

She went on. "You thought you could tell what real love is, but you couldn't. In all your life the best loving you said you ever had turns out to be fake. How wonderful that must make you feel."

I was very sad and my voice broke with the emotion. "Do you really think that's a great thing, being able to fake love so well that I was fooled deep down in my soul?"

I looked away from her up the road and I could see two sets of flashing red lights headed towards us but still several miles away.

She couldn't miss them either.

"You lost out, Jackie. People really can love each other. You put on quite an act. You were like an actress playing Desdemona so well the character came more alive than the actress herself. You think you cheated me and you're clever. But it's not so."

We were looking at each other again and her eyes looked into mine, first one, and then the other. And the hate I saw there burned into me. She waved the pistol at me.

"Tell me this isn't so," she screamed at me.

I could see my death in her eyes.

She squeezed the trigger. Twice. The gun clicked but nothing happened. It was empty. I was still alive. I grabbed the gun and twisted it out of her hand. I threw the stupid thing as far as I could.

I shouted at her. "I'm the one left with emotions, with loss and regret. You're left with nothing."

Jackie came at me with both hands like claws, scratching, biting. I grabbed at her wrists but she was too quick and I was too weak. But, as she pounded at my nose, I found the flasher button on the steering column and pushed it in. I deliberately elbowed the horn again and again as I attempted to push her away from me.

Then a policeman was at the window shouting and Jackie bent over into the seat and wailed like an animal hunted down and cornered.

The cops took Jackie and they and the ambulance followed me to the house. The ambulance took Bruce Scarf away to the hospital. The police were about to take Jackie away when she asked to speak to me privately. At my request the police consented.

We stood under the white-blossomed apple tree away from Carol and the policemen. Her hands were cuffed behind her.

She smiled and her eyes were moist with tragedy as I remembered them when she first sat down across from me at the Balcony Restaurant. But her smile never broke as she leaned so close that it must have seemed to Carol that Jackie was kissing me good-bye.

She wasn't.

"I don't want you to forget me, Jay. Here's something to always keep me in your head."

She leaned into me and twisted to show me something small in one hand. She nodded to me to take it. I did and looked at it and thought she had given me a tiny doll. Then I recognized it for the little finger from a human hand. Harry's.

She walked quickly away and slid into the backseat of the police car without looking at me again. I turned away and, carrying Harry's finger, walked rapidly across the lawn around the house to the bay. Carol followed behind me.

"Jay, stop. Where are you going?"

I threw Harry's finger as far as I could and heard it splash like a small stone out with the hermit crabs and other sea scavengers. Then I turned back to Carol. She put her arms around me and buried her face in my shoulder. She was crying. I started to cry too.

"What was it?" Carol asked.

"Nothing. It was nothing."